The
Drum

By

Anthony Ashpitel

ISBN 978-0-9569003-3-3

Published by Anthony Ashpitel
Email: tonyashpitel@btinternet.com

Updated in 2011 from an original novel by Anthony Ashpitel

THE DRUM

This book is dedicated to my wife, Anne, who is a
boundless source of help and encouragement.

AA

ANTHONY ASHPITEL

Chapter One

As the heavy lorry trundled down the rough country road, the rattles and squeaks reverberated off the metal walls of the cab with the decibel level of an average discotheque at warm-up. However, for all that the driver noticed it might have been as quiet as the grave; as quiet, but not as calm. Moreover, the reason for this seeming paradox was that the driver was sweating and twisting as he fought to control the vehicle along the pot-holed surface. No momentary loss of concentration could be allowed if he, the vehicle, and his dangerous cargo were to avoid the crumbling edge, which fell away steeply to the River Breck below.

He had made the trip many times but he never failed to experience that feeling of dread that made his stomach freeze at the start of each journey. Equally, he had never failed to curse the stupidity of anyone who would position a chemical factory in the Pennines proper and forget to spend the necessary thought time and money on a safe road to take the chemical products and waste out into civilisation.

He was almost at the bottom of the long descent now and approaching the greatest hurdle before he got onto the far better A-road just outside Wicklees. The obstacle was a bridge, one perfectly ample for the traffic of a hundred years ago

5

but almost impassable for the thirty-two ton vehicles that now regularly squeezed over its pronounced hump. In the brief respite, which his approach allowed, he had time only to wipe his brow with the sleeve of his sodden shirt before returning his full concentration to the twist of potholed tarmac ahead.

It was as his gaze swept ahead to the bridge itself that something in the water beneath caught his eye. In his eyes for one brief millisecond, he wore the look of recognition but the message never reached his brain because it was already selecting only that data that would help fulfil the plan he was working upon: crossing the bridge in one piece.

Because of this, he didn't recognise the green semi-cylindrical object for what it was. And even were he to have had longer to look upon it from his cab it is doubtful he could have seen the real danger there. It would have required a far slower approach, far longer gaze, and a vantage much closer, to understand the significance of what was there to be seen.

As the big lorry grunted and groaned its way up the incline beyond the bridge the driver had time to remember that something had drawn his attention earlier and look back to see what it was. But the bridge was just out of view now as a gnarled and stunted tree obscured that part of the moor.

Just about the time he looked back, again to coax the lorry up the hill the semi-cylindrical object was receiving the attention of another being. The kestrel had waited for the lorry to pass before cruising in to land on the rim beyond the curved surface. It then spent a few seconds looking around. One end of the object was in the water while the other had sunk in the slimy mud at the water's edge. Blending with the roar of the river was the trickle of black liquid pouring from a hole in the object. Around on the bank lay a collection of creatures devoid of life. Downstream a vole lay half in and half out of the water, eyes bulging and mouth formed as if poised to scream only that scream which the severest sensation of pain can bring. Now it would never utter another sound.

It had been a massacre; the only difference in the demise of the collection of animals beneath the watching kestrel and the vole downstream being that they had died a more pleasant death through breathing in the aerosol vapours from the drum in a far more diluted form and therefore escaping the violent spasm of mortal pain suffered by the vole.

The kestrel cried out then, sensing the danger at last. But it was too late. She had barely left her slippery perch, her wings clawing at the air in a frantic bid to flee, when control was lost and she nose-dived into the coarse grass. For a few seconds she continued to beat her wings, not realising what was happening. Then, after a brief pause, the body convulsed once more and lay still.

Only a few feet away, the half-submerged drum continued to trickle out its potion of death, physically no different to the sixty-or-so other drums which were lashed atop the lorry still struggling up the hill, whose driver was still swearing at the stupidity of people who...

Later that morning, and some miles downstream, a birthday picnic had just begun. Overhead, the sun peeked cautiously from between the clouds of a September sky with increasing frequency and hopes for the planned swim were high. So it was that twenty-two children of primary school age skipped gleefully down the long sloping rear lawns of the *George Inn* to the edge of the now placid waters of the River Breck. Away up the slope towards the inn and well away from the garden tables populated by the drinking patrons, several nannies fussed over the aftermath of the twenty-two quick-change artists and began laying out the picnic.

Occasionally, each nanny would turn to watch the antics of the children and the two minders as they frolicked about in the water. From the tables nearer the inn they could hear the chuckles of other onlookers.

A young nanny called Anne watched with the rest, happily sharing what the recent heavy rains seemed to indicate was the last swim of the season. Not that her young charge would worry too much at that: he was not overly fond of swimming, much preferring the drier prospect other sports such as football afforded.

Thinking of this prompted her to look towards the group in the river. There was a lot of splashing going on and it was difficult to make out some of the figures but, after careful study, she knew he was not with them. With the lurch of panic that accompanied this conclusion, she turned to the other nannies that were still giggling and chattering.

Her fear must have shown in her eyes for one of the other women stopped talking and looked over to her.

'Something the matter, dear?' she said, moving towards Anne.

Anne looked wildly about her before she replied. 'It's Toby. I can't see him. He's not with the others.'

The older woman smiled at this and placed a calming hand on Arm's arm. 'That's because he's not in the water. He's behind you, further down the bank.'

At this, Anne let out a sigh of relief and made to run over to Toby who was quietly watching the others but the older woman's hand restrained her.

'Don't worry,' she said, 'We're all keeping our eyes open.'

'All except me, it seems,' replied Anne, and gave a weak smile.

Hardly had her relief subsided when it was replaced with concern for the boy again, this time because she knew he was shy and took a while to become involved in these things. But then, even as she looked, he began to move along the grass towards the shrieking group. With a similar resolve to that shown by the boy, Anne dismissed her concern and decided determinedly that she was going to enjoy this outing.

Anne's enjoyment lasted only seconds until, like everyone else, she involuntarily froze in response to the piercing scream from the river. With the rest of the onlookers, she strove to search out the reason for the girl's agonising cry. At first she could see nothing amiss; the group were still playing, though somewhat subdued, and her little boy still hadn't made it into the water. But, otherwise, there was nothing untoward.

Then she saw that which had the men at the other tables running furiously towards the river. One of the attending girls in the river was supporting two children, both of whom seemed asleep. The other girl was supporting two more until she too collapsed, carrying the others with her. Then all around the other children began to slip down into the water. Not another scream was uttered from the group, not a cry or a whimper, just collective unconsciousness. The nannies, transfixed in shock, stared unbelievingly at the sight.

It was some moments before Anne recovered and joined the others in rushing to help. The men were already in the water and dragging the children to the bank with a roughness demanded by the need for haste if the children weren't to drown. Then it was up to the collected crowd to tend the frail little bodies until the ambulances arrived.

It was only minutes before the first one arrived and it was soon leading a convoy of cars commandeered for use in ferrying the rest of the children. Every child - and one of the attending girls - was taken to hospital. Every one of these was now unconscious.

There had been no room for Anne in the car that had taken Toby away. A policeman told her that they would have transport for those remaining in just a little while and while she waited, she answered the few questions asked of her, feeling dazed and unreal. She began to shiver and all around seemed darker now. Automatically she looked up at the sky and discovered that it wasn't just her present mood that was black, the sky had also taken on a similar hue and the first spots of rain began to fall.

At about the same time that the young girl had screamed the telephone on the desk of a London national newspaper began to ring, startling the reporter out of his reverie. For all the shock to his nervous system this caused, he was grateful for the diversion the call would bring. He had spent several hours penning his weekly thousand words on the environment and had been of the writer's malady for most of them.

His feeling of expectancy as he reached for the phone meant he was indeed in bad creative state for all that he had come to expect from the telephone was abuse from his editor and a number of crank calls. It took only seconds for him to feel that his luck had not changed for the better as he listened to the cultured voice of the man at the other end.

Nor did he have long to assess the call for only one sentence was spoken, albeit repeated twice. After several entreaties for the caller to identify himself - to no avail - the reporter hung up. For all that, the conversation had lasted twenty-five seconds he was still the last one to stop talking. It is wasteful of time and effort to talk into an instrument whose only activity is a regular electronic purring, he reflected, replacing the receiver.

The reporter was used to crank calls, either from those who objected to his investigations of environmental hazards as much as from those who meant to settle personal scores by slagging-off those in charge of environmental 'health'. Only one thing was universally common, he knew; all such calls were made anonymously.

However, he had once or twice found grounds for substantiating such allegations and it was for this reason that he had faithfully followed up every call. This time was no exception and, as he glanced at what he had written down during the call, he reached for the computer keyboard and tried a search on the internet. Failing to elicit instant gratification, he reached for the internal telephone.

While he waited for 'Research' to answer, he savoured the message, 'Ask John Arrowsmith about pollution of the River Breck,' was all it said. He couldn't place the name as being significant, in Public Health or similar departments or in anything else for that matter. Nor could he place the River Breck. It was a prime case for 'Research' and he fed this information to the man answering the internal phone.

Then he looked down again at the scrappy mess that was meant to be the outline of a factual, punishing attack on the state of Britain's environmental Eco-structure and sighed deeply for the umpteenth time that morning. It was no use, he realised; he was getting nowhere. He decided it was time to do his own research, that great standby of those momentarily bereft of creativity. The time was eleven-fifteen, as noted on his short transcript of the anonymous telephone call, so the object of his research might just as well involve the public bar of The Swan.

Chapter Two

In the Council Chamber of Wicklees Town Hall, the portraits of countless former local dignitaries stared down on those present in real life. Surrounded by a Victorian's idea of all that was best in décor most of those assembled there just four and a half hours after the picnic incident felt as though they were impostors. In the main that was the case, for it was only a desire to be closer to the incident that had driven the Area Health Authority to hold its emergency meeting here.

Elsewhere, other emergency meetings were taking place. The council had already had theirs, just three hours ago in this chamber. It had been then that the Public Health department had tabled its assessment and intentions regarding the incident and other interested local government departments had also been heard.

However, beyond the normal emergency hospital services, no strategic medical plan for this particular incident had been hammered out. That would be the task of the AHA and, though it had taken four and a half hours for all its members to assemble through their being more widely located over the area, there was no lack of immediacy in their resolve to attack the medical problems facing them.

They were not all medical men. Even the chairman, a tall, dignified man, whose eyes of gleaming intelligence didn't always match the air of bonhomie invariably conjured up by the rest of his facial features, was a businessman. It had been his efficiency as a leader and a wily one at that which had overridden the claims of medical men for a medical chairman and swayed a Secretary of State for Health, years ago, to exercise his prerogative in selecting this man. Successive Secretaries of State had endorsed the selection so that he was now known, almost by everyone, as the 'Chairman'.

Of the remaining twenty AHA members, for not all present were of that body, a third had been appointed by the medical profession, another one third by local authorities, and the final third again by the Secretary of State. Hence, several of those at the earlier Council meeting were again present. In addition, two other people were present; the squire, Lord Alland, whose expression of utter resignation was in complete contrast to his normal mien, and, Inspector Davies, a CID man from the local police force.

The grave tones of the speakers rebounded hollowly off the panelled walls of the small chamber as each member with any knowledge of the incident recounted it for the benefit of the rest. Occasionally the Chairman would interrupt with a question to demonstrate his hold on the proceedings and then allow a speaker to pick up where they had left off.

Presently the time came for the Chairman to put all the facts together and give his usual summation. He was famous for this, always balancing evidence against speculation and presenting the result in a concise and logical fashion. It was almost as if he were the judge, the other members the jury, and many would say that he had missed his vocation by deserting the study of law for business on the very brink of being called to the bar as a young man.

'Of course, at this early stage there is so much to be discovered before we can decide upon the causative agent but, as Mr Wagstaff has told us,' he acknowledged the Public Health man, 'his department are scouring the area upstream of the incident site and may give us a result before we hear from the laboratories…'

As he spoke his eyes gazed in turn at each person, ignoring only the secretary, and not for the first time he saw something in the eyes of Lord Alland that disturbed him. He saw something else in those eyes other than the feeling of sympathy and concern they all shared for those who had been poisoned. Alland seemed to have shrunk in stature both physically and mentally. He seemed to be a man whose spirit was crushed and this observation worried the Chairman more than a little.

He had known Lord Alland for several years, having served on a number of boards as a fellow director. They had even been friends until lately when Alland had seemed to avoid him. Just why he should suddenly change hadn't yet been explained.

Knowing something of the man's past didn't throw any light onto the question of why the incident should have caused such a profound collapse of spirit. The opposite would be nearer the mark for here was a man who had not only proved in Aden that he possessed both an iron nerve and will, but had seen misery on a much larger scale as a major in bomb disposal during the 'Troubles.'

Such thoughts made the Chairman wonder if there were truth in believing that the older one became the softer was the stomach for misery. He supposed it depended how personal was the misery. Perhaps Alland's present state of mind had nothing to do with such notions, but simply to do with his reason for being at the meetings: his being the owner of the land on which the incident had occurred.

Such thoughts did not interfere with his summation. Indeed such was the brevity in the time it had taken for his brain to think these thoughts that not only had he only been aware of the emotion concerned, his subconscious taking care of the rest, he had not progressed one word further in what he was saying.

'…Such chemical analysis is a tedious business, I'm told, and though one shouldn't pre-empt the results, it would seem to me that we are dealing here with an incident of negligence in the disposal of toxic waste.'

The many grave nods from around the long table assured him that this was the general conclusion and he saw no reason not to go one stage further in his speculation and gain a political point or two at the same time. True, there were no reporters present; in fact, the story had been blocked to avoid erroneous publicity until the situation was better known - but eventually the record of this meeting might become public and it was as well to have one's stance known from the start.

'The next question is, I fear, whether the presence of a toxic substance in the River Breck was deliberate or accidental,' he continued, and his expression was grave.

'A trifle premature these observations may be but we must bear in mind that deliberate waste dumping, or negligence - and I view both as being the same thing - is on the increase and...' At this point, he stopped and allowed a weak smile to grace his lips. 'But enough of such speculation, we must await the facts.'

He had made his point. The bit about viewing negligence had made his point. The bit about viewing negligence and deliberate waste dumping the same way was now on the secretary's recording machine and therefore on record; whatever came out of all this, his stance was known.

Again, he looked around the group of faces. 'Is there anything anyone would like to add at this stage?'

There may well have been urgent questions or information on the lips of some of those present but for the moment at least they could only bide their time. The reason for this was a scene that took all of them by surprise. No sooner had the Chairman asked his question than the two large ornate doors parted and the assembled people heard the sound of angry voices approaching.

By far the loudest of the voices was the cause of more surprise in the members, as the owner of it could not have been a more unlikely match. It was the nanny, Anne, who burst white-faced but loudly into the Council Chamber, with the Chairman's personal assistant making ineffectual attempts to both physically hold her back and persuade her vocally against her action.

It said something for the Chairman's acumen that he read the situation as if the two people had entered with six-foot placards in their hands. His actions were almost as instantaneous, too. With a wave of one of his elongated hands, he dismissed his PA while telling him to close the door behind him.

Then he turned his attention to the girl, his manner now sympathetic. 'My dear, whatever is the matter?'

He didn't wait for an answer because he was turning to those sat at the table in which direction he aimed a sharper look to that shown to the girl. 'Collins. A chair for the young lady.'

As Anne sat down, aware now of the reality of facing so many inquisitive glances, the words failed to come.

'You were present at the incident?' asked the Chairman, helpfully.

The girl cleared her throat, the anger that had lent her courage to break into the meeting seeming to have never existed. 'Yes, I was, sir.'

'And you wish to know just what is happening.' The Chairman's tones belied the sarcastic interpretation felt by the others but not the girl. They could sense that he would go so far to help the girl state her business with the politeness of a defending counsel to his client, but should he realise that she was wasting his time he would pounce and rather heavily at that. The others saw the signs.

The girl nodded then shook her head. 'No, I'm not stupid,' she cried. 'I realise you can't know all the answers yet.'

'Thank you for allowing us to be human, Miss…'

The girl's face cleared then and the hue of her face returned to that she had worn on entering the room. She hadn't missed the Chairman's sarcasm this time. 'Miss Metcalfe,' she provided, her voice now flat. 'My reason for being here is to ask a very pertinent question.'

'And that is?'

'In a moment,' she riposted, stunned at her own audacity. 'First, I need to know why you have instructed all concerned to a vow of silence.'

'Quite simply to avoid panic and dangerous speculation. In a few hours we will make a statement of our findings,' he returned. Then his eyes and face matched in icy contemplation that of the girl before him. 'Which everyone else but you is happy to wait for!'

'Then what about the story you told them: that the cause was some, er, toxic substance in the river?'

'Merely the truth.'

'How do you come to that conclusion?'

The Chairman looked around the assembled members. Then he shook his head unbelievingly and said, thinking aloud, 'How do we come to that conclusion.' He turned back to the girl. 'Because, young lady, everyone who went into the river later fell into unconsciousness and showed signs of poisoning. That is why! And if you must waste the time....'

He fell silent then because he became aware that the girl was shaking her head vigorously and saying something. He asked her to repeat what she had said.

'I just said that your statement is untrue. For a start, twenty-three people became unconscious...'

'That is correct,' interrupted the Chairman. 'I have the figures here; twenty-two children and one adult, an attendant. Twenty-three people go into the water and twenty-three people are poisoned. Wouldn't you say that was strong case for saying that they were poisoned because of something toxic in the river water?'

A murmur of sycophantic merriment went round the table.

'It would if your facts were correct.'

For the first time the Chairman's pace was checked. He wouldn't have been able to explain exactly why but it was probably because the girl had remained steadfast when anyone less sure of their ground, male or female, would have bolted. 'You were there, Miss Metcalfe. You tell us what you believe to be the facts.'

In the next few minutes, interrupted occasionally by the Chairman's usual steering questions, she recounted what had happened. She spoke of her charge's reluctance to enter the water, pointing out that he had nevertheless succumbed to the poison, and of the presence of a second adult in the water who had not lapsed into unconsciousness. She added the observation that none of the men who had gone into the water had suffered any symptoms of poisoning.

When she had finished she became aware of a new respect among the circle of faces and, for a few moments, even the Chairman was silent. But not for long.

'As I see it,' he began, 'we can either believe that the poison was all around, or administered to the bathers before the swim, or we can believe the toxin was in the river. The young lady here has of course placed doubts in the path of following the latter theory but I feel that neither of the others stands up under the same testing criteria.

'We have, it seems, a problem of elimination. On the first count, that of poisoning through administration, we should need to know if all twenty-three - but only those twenty-three - drank or ate the same substances prior to entering the water. At the outset, I believe we can dispense with that for reasons I shall come to in a moment. On the second point, that of whether the poison was all around - on the trees, on the grass as well as in the water - similarly fails to stand up to even casual scrutiny because only the twenty-three succumbed to poisoning.'

He paused then to look toward the door where the PA now stood. In his hand, he held an envelope and he brought it across the room at the Chairman's signal. As the PA turned to go the Chairman resumed speaking, ignoring for the moment the envelope placed in front of him.

'The third theory, the one we adopted unanimously until Miss Metcalfe came along, fails under the same test of criteria. We are speaking about water. Let that be understood. I understand certain chemicals are far more readily absorbed by being taken orally. Add these two points together in considering what happened and I think you will find our unanimous decision reinstated.'

The Chairman then turned to face the girl. 'When you said your little boy didn't go into the river and therefore couldn't have been poisoned I was prepared to believe you. I still am. But then you said you didn't see him all the time - that another nanny had to point out his location to you. Now I don't believe he was in the water while out of your sight but I do believe he could have been grubbing around the wet bank in the manner of every youngster of his age. And likely he'd put his fingers to his mouth from time to time, as well.'

At his questioning glance, the girl nodded her head at the truth in his statement.

'As regards the woman in the water who wasn't poisoned, surely it is possible that no particle of water passed her lips even though there was a lot of splashing. And couldn't the same reasoning apply to that of the men who ran into the water and brought the children ashore? Or, possibly, the poison had passed down river by the time they entered. I think therefore that I, for one, will remain loyal to our first conclusion, gentlemen...and lady.'

As the Chairman belatedly opened the envelope, a murmur of assent passed around the table, even the girl allowing a nod of her head. Then the Chairman was looking up from the note he had read and leaning towards the girl. 'I do appreciate the sincerity of your mission here. I have here in my hand the confirmation of what we suspected and now must discuss its implications with my colleagues. Would you excuse us?'

With a brief instruction to one of the younger members, he had the girl escorted to the door. Then he turned to address the board members. 'This is it, Gentlemen. Though I suspect the message should really have been presented to you, Holland. Apart from the fact that the source was a forty-five gallon drum which was located in the river some way upstream from the site the rest is just unpronounceable gibberish to me.' With that he handed the piece of paper to the man he had addressed.

After one brief look, the man's expression changed. It wasn't for the better, either.

'Perhaps you would share your thoughts with the rest of us,' urged the Chairman.

The man looked up quickly, his free hand whipping away the spectacles he wore low on the curve of his nose. 'It is a short message to say that they have found the source of the pollutant and that it is a herbicide substance with a concentration of no more than nought point one parts per million at the incident site.'

'And what does that mean - in layman's terms?'

'That the concentration just measured is almost negligible.'

'Does that mean there is now no risk of recurrence?' asked the inspector.

'It does indeed,' replied the holder of the letter, a forensics man.

'Then why your reaction?' asked the Chairman. 'You looked as if you'd seen a ghost.'

The forensics man fingered his tie nervously. 'In a way I had. The name on this piece of paper is that of a substance which is at once too valuable to society and too expensive.'

'You can skip the philosophy, Holland. Just tell us what it is and if those children will be all right.'

'Of course, sir,' he answered, his tone business-like. 'The chemical named on this paper is 2,4,5-T. It is a very effective herbicide used widely around the world. To have caused the symptoms we have seen in the children - and I am recalling from memory here - it would have required a concentration many times greater than our reading shows. However, it may be that the pollution wasn't equally dispersed and that - four-hours ago - the concentration was much higher. As we have seen through clinical observation of the patients, they have ingested a much higher dose of the substance than these readings indicated. Just how high won't be known for some time, however.'

'What are the symptoms of poisoning by this substance? Are they the same as those we have seen?' This from the Public Health man.

'Those we have seen so far - that is, rapid list-lessness followed by unconsciousness - certainly follow the same pattern.'

He paused then, knowing that what he had not yet said was what his listeners really wanted to hear. 'As for the symptoms we can expect to see if it is poisoning by this substance, you must realise it depends on the dosage. It may be that they will recover completely with good hospital practice with no signs of their ordeal apart from a long sleep.'

'What is the other possibility?' This from the police inspector.

Holland sighed. 'Ventricular fibrillation, I should think. Possibly cardiac arrest, with or without the fibrillation. And death,' he said, and then added quickly, 'Of course, I am reciting from memory.'

'But you think you might be right about the death bit,' this again from the inspector.

'Yes. But that would depend on the dose taken, which in turn depends upon the size of the person.'

'And the smaller the person - a young child being a small person - the smaller the dose required.'

'Yes.'

'But is this two-four whatsit freely available in this country when it is so dangerous?'

'2,4,5-T. Trichlorophenoxacetic acid,' corrected Holland. 'Yes, it's freely available.'

The inspector was obviously getting at something for he spoke again. 'Why then did you say it was too expensive as if you meant too expensive for the world? And why did you react when you first saw it?'

'Inspector Davies!' cried the Chairman. 'Let us concentrated our qualified expertise on the problem at hand. Which is: ensuring that this incident is dealt with to the best preservation of life. Then we can worry about the wider issues.'

'I'm sorry,' responded the inspector, without the emotion of apology reaching his voice. 'But I will have to deploy a few of my hard-pressed men on this case - men I can ill-afford to spare anyway with our activities surrounding that damned pop concert - so it would help me estimate the man-power required if I knew the information I have asked for.'

The Chairman looked over to the forensics man. 'Go ahead, please.'

'You wanted to know why I was alarmed?' began Holland. 'Well, quite simply, I misread the name. Instead of what I have since read out, I thought it was another substance 2,3,7,8-T. Tri-chlorodibenzo-para-dioxin. Otherwise known as TCDD. It is another kettle of fish altogether. But as I say, I misread it, so comment on TCDD is not relevant.'

'Then perhaps we can get on with our real business,' said the Chairman, shortly.

But again, he was to be temporarily thwarted by the bleep of the telephone in front of him. It was the PA, with a message that the press were on the line and wished to speak only to him. The Chairman's reaction to this was that of one worn down by continual interruptions and he viewed the seeming leak of the story to the press with the resignation of one who had been silly to hope against hope anyway.

At the end of the short telephone conversation that followed, the Chairman's mien was not as it was at the start. With indignation in his voice, he repeated what the reporter had said.

He had been right to put on record his feelings about pollution for it seemed that either someone wanted to get at him directly or wished to draw his attention to the illegal operations of someone else. Either way, he would have to be very canny in his future actions.

'Gentlemen,' he said, slowly, 'it seems someone has called a national newspaper with the cryptic message: "Ask me, er John Arrowsmith, about the pollution of the River Breck."'

As the murmur of voices subsided, the Chairman spoke again, 'Also, whoever it was wouldn't leave his name. I suppose it is the norm in such cases.' He turned to the policeman. 'What do you think, Inspector?'

'Could be a crank. I'll look into it as with everything else concerning the incident.'

'And so will I,' said the Chairman, and pressed a button on the telephone.

Seconds later, when he had replaced the receiver, he looked up and addressed the inspector. 'You've said your men are already overworked. I intend to remove some of the load. We have a man investigating industrial pollution at the moment. I know because he is working on factories in our area. It can only be to our advantage to have an expert on the scene.'

The inspector nodded. 'With the normal reservations, I must agree.' He reached for his notebook. 'Do you have a name, sir?'

The Chairman looked down at the name he had just scribbled onto the pad. 'Certainly. David Black.'

Chapter Three

George Appleton stared out of the window at the rain-lashed lawn that sloped down to the river. Behind him, he could occasionally hear the sounds of staff in the other rooms as they cleared away the debris of the lunchtime session. But there was no-one else in the bar. He was alone; there was just himself and his thoughts.

It was now difficult to believe the tragedy had occurred at all: to visualize as ever being real that scene which still caused his heart to quicken; of the sudden cessation of laughter, the scream, and the ensuing chaos. Perhaps the premature darkening of the landscape that had come with the downpour was the obstacle to this mental reconciliation, the sunny outlook of a few hours before being replaced by one of brooding.

He was a burly man, balding fast and recently become lazy. He had been landlord at the *George Inn* for two years, and unlikely to stay much longer when the brewery owners had taken a look at his latest books. They had warned him of his managerial deficiencies but he knew he couldn't change, he was too old and set in his ways for that. It had been a mistake to come here in the first place. The odd thing was, he didn't care.

He had been in the beer trade all of his adult life apart from time spent in the army in the early 'fifties. In the main, he had been employed in town public houses, used to the faster pace of life there. But after they had bulldozed his last pub as part of a redevelopment scheme, he had had to consider other offers. Now he was in a country inn, feeding occasional passers-by and selling them rooms.

The new life didn't suit him. The extra responsibility of running the restaurant and rooms, in which he'd had no real experience, made the whole life a job of work instead of the hobby it had once been. Like so many thousands of other people who plodded through their daily toil, he had lost interest and was now enduring a job of work he no longer enjoyed.

So much had his new position affected him that he shied away from any work other than the bar where, feeling on safe ground, he felt happiest. Often he would retreat to it as a place of sanctuary, as he had now.

It may have been several minutes before his staring eyes saw the figure out on the lawn. His first reaction was that the man was an idiot for he was stood well clear of the nearest, sheltering tree and the rain was cascading off his head and down his overcoat. As Appleton watched the man's every movement, he decided he must be looking for something as he was never stationary or even upright for long and at each few steps would crouch to prod at the short grass.

Within seconds Appleton's interest had turned to suspicion for surely not even idiots stayed out in such weather without good reason. Perhaps the man's presence had something to do with the tragedy. Perhaps he was connected with the cause in some way. It was then that he broke a rule which he had kept for many years, a rule which though totally unreasonable was inbred through close proximity to people whose beery talk was as persuasive and wise as their own regard for law was uncommon. He called the police.

Within two minutes he was back at the window, noticeably out of breath from his short but rushed journey to the telephone behind the bar. The man was still there, still mooching about and seemingly oblivious to the awful weather. But would he stay here until the police arrived? This was the publican's main worry at that moment and, fearing that the man's business in such a featureless area couldn't keep him there much longer, he concentrated on compiling a description of him.

With the distance between them all of twenty-five yards, and the light not at all good, the figure was somewhat blurred. He was about six-feet tall - that was easy-to see - and he was of slim build even allowing for the limp overcoat. Beyond that, description was more difficult.

At that range, it was difficult to make out the features beneath the flattened mop of dark hair but once, when the man looked directly at the inn, Appleton got a better look. It was a rugged face with a stubborn chin and wide jaw and the neck that jutted out of the upturned collar was thick and muscular. Appleton guessed the man to be in his late thirties, and got the overall impression that here was a man in the peak of fitness. At that moment, the face merely registered mild curiosity, but having seen the most complete cross-section of humanity it is possible to see in one man's life-time, the fat publican knew this was a man on whose side it was better to be rather than against.

Then he saw three men join the lone figure and sighed with relief. It was the local inspector and two of his constables. As they spoke animatedly, Appleton gazed on. Soon they turned and began walking towards the inn. Within a minute he could hear them entering by the main door.

As he went out into the foyer, the four men were putting down irregular shaped pieces of cus-tomised luggage, all of which were in the same black fibre material. Then the plain-clothes po-liceman came over, moving him away from the others. 'It's all right, George,' he said. 'He's a sci-entist, something to do with the incident this morning.'

'Come to take samples and things, has he?' re-plied George, still eyeing the man with suspicion.

'Something like that. I gather he wants a room here. Look after him will you?'

'He'll get the same treatment as everyone else gets.'

'Yes,' agreed Inspector Davies, used to Ap-pleton's prickly temperament by now. 'Thanks for the call.'

With that, the inspector turned to the two uniformed policemen. 'Right lads, I'll see you later at the station.' Then he was gone, banging the front door behind him.

It took only seconds for the stranger to learn that a room was available and receive a key. However, in that time the publican discovered one more feature that he could have included in the now unnecessary description: the man's eyes. They were the deepest brown eyes he had ever seen, not that he was in the habit of looking into those of complete strangers, especially males, but he had learned that if there is one thing that tells you most about a person it is their eyes. When he had been treated to the one level glance of those smoky orbs he knew they belonged to a man who would not profitably be tangled with. Appleton decided it would be best to avoid Mr Black, starting now. With brief directions on how to get to his room, the publican left him and returned to the bar.

For a few moments, David Black didn't move from his position close to the tiny reception desk. He was now alone, the two uniformed policemen having already left quietly. Patiently he dabbed away the water from his face with a handkerchief before stooping to pick up the two largest cases from the heap of luggage. Then he began to climb the stairs.

He had made three short trips and was descending the stairs to collect the last pair of bags when he noticed the young waitress. His immediate impression was that she had somehow stumbled into such employ by chance as her bearing and careful attention to appearance clashed with the uniform she wore tightly about her lithe figure.

In the few seconds he watched unnoticed, this theory was strengthened by the fact that she was wandering around the foyer, seemingly confused by the number of doors, while feeling she must make a choice. Then there came the sound of laughter from behind the door to the bar and she turned to open it.

Black's pace had merely slowed on first sighting the girl, having been taken slightly aback by her good looks as much as her obvious predicament. But when she opened the door, he stopped, as if he had walked into a brick wall. The reason had nothing to do with the girl this time, his action caused by hearing what the opened door allowed him to hear.

'...of course it is a secret and I'll ask you to keep mum about it,' said a voice, which abruptly halted.

Then there was a moment's pause followed by, in another voice, 'Oh, come in, Rose. Our new barmaid, Gentlemen.'

With that, the door shut behind the girl, muffling the words from within. Quickly, Black moved over to the door and pressed an ear against it. But whatever he was expecting to hear didn't materialize for after a minute he gave up, his knowledge increased only by the news that the girl was so new she had only started that afternoon.

In room eighteen David Black was surveying his home from home with interest, not to say downright suspicion. Nothing untoward prompted this intense emotion; it was just a product of his way of life. As hotel rooms went it was quite well appointed, with a bathroom en suite to supplement the international standard of twin beds, and an electronic headboard complete with radio and clock. On the mirrored dressing-table, beside the built-in wardrobe, stood a small colour television and a telephone, and a small folding card announcing 'Wi-Fi' connectivity and the passkey.

The floor space, however, was quite restricted and he spent the next minute-or-so organising his heavy cases into a neat group where they might least interfere with his progress around the room. Then from the last one he withdrew an electric shaver, which also had with it a battery charger. Outwardly, it was no different from the more expensive battery-mains devices and Black was quite impressed with the closeness of shave it gave in addition to its other designed requirement. This latter was to run up and down the shortwave band of radio frequencies transmitting on each one in turn. It had a range of no more than ten yards but was quite adequate for its purpose; that of scrambler to any conversation held within the radius of its influence. It didn't totally drown out any bugging device but by transmitting on each frequency at least once every millisecond, it was enough to deny an electronically-aided eavesdropper of any success whatsoever.

His first task was to check-in with his temporary boss and so he picked up the telephone to call him. By doing so he purposely eschewed use of his mobile phone, a device that, in Black's opinion, was akin to opening your window and shouting yours and your correspondent's conversation to the entire world, such is the level of security it provides. To the ungodly, he knew by bitter experience from previous missions, only simple electronics are required to intercept conversation by mobile phone, assuming they are not using your mobile phone as a bugging device on your non-telephonic conversations.

Black was used to not working with such a device, carrying his in a special cloth, normally switched off – battery disconnected by a special switch - which contained a micro-mesh of copper strands to prevent any electronic 'interference' going in or out of the device. He found carrying one of his admittedly special phones, that contained a scrambler app, could also be counter-productive. This was because the ungodly, monitoring such a device, would be in receipt of a garbled message that couldn't be mistaken with simple interference. At the very least they would then know that the operative using such a device was no, in his case, innocent scientist and would also know his location. None of this meant he never used the device. It was just that he was careful, very careful, and would strive to at least use a different phone mast to where he expected eavesdroppers to be, as only the major intelligence services could monitor and interrogate the entire network.

Within the next few minutes he learned a few things quite apart from what the Chairman had said. He discovered the telephone was connected to the exchange through a switchboard downstairs and that whoever connected him to the outside world had spent the whole of the conversation listening in. What he didn't know was that it was the girl from the bar who had responded to the buzzer and who, after connecting him, had made copious notes of what was said. Nor did he know that after he had rung off she had checked the number called with directory enquiries and then phoned someone else with a *résumé* of what had transpired.

However, the fact that someone had eavesdropped over a telephone line was not something that worried Black unduly. It was natural that his arrival at such short notice after the incident should arouse a certain curiosity. It was plain human nature, he knew. He also knew that the fact he had heard the sharp click at all told him it was no professional intercepting his conversation. And it was unimportant either way as it had only been a check-in call and from then on the contents of his large cases would dissuade any further interceptions by this means.

It took him no longer than fifteen minutes to wash and change from his sodden clothes. Then when he had hung the wet clothes from a makeshift line in the bathroom, he quickly tidied up the room. After a final glance around to make sure nothing was amiss, he turned for the door and was soon padding the deep carpeting of the corridor on his way out.

The foyer was again deserted when he got there but he could still hear muffled voices from behind the bar door. On his way out of the front entrance, he checked and turned back, then strode over to the Bar and opened the door.

There were four people at the bar, Appleton, the girl and the two policemen. Away in the corner and lounging around one of the tables were two rather scruffy men.

'Excuse me, Landlord,' called Black, as the conversation at the bar ceased abruptly. In the corner the two men continued oblivious to his presence.

'Yes?' responded Appleton.

'What time does dinner begin?'

'Any time after six - until nine.'

'Thanks.' With that Black left, closing the door behind him. To know the time of Dinner had been a plausible excuse for entering the bar, but the real reason had been to match faces to the voices he had heard when the girl had opened the door earlier. He hadn't succeeded completely in this as he still didn't know who had been telling the 'secret' but it was pretty certain to have been one of those he had just seen.

During the next few hours Black drove his estate car to the addresses on the list he had scribbled in his notebook. Each address was either a producer or user of toxic chemicals. It was a short list, covering an area of seventy square miles of country where farms far outnumbered industrial premises. The list could have been much longer had such farms, users of many toxic chemicals in the form of herb and pesticides, been added. Fortunately the Department of Agriculture were looking after that aspect, while he concentrated on source and large consumers.

He had been in the job for some months now, investigating industrial pollution in general and incidents of toxic dumping in particular. Not for him was slavish adherence to the bureaucratic dictates of the Health and Safety Executive. He believed they and their masters in Europe had really lost the plot when it came to formulating and carrying out risk-based solutions policy. He was annoyed when he reflected upon the pantheon of edicts emanating from such organisations which effectively banned everyone from doing anything on the basis that something might, just might, well it possibly could, happen. Basic laws already covered the health and safety environment, he believed and, in his opinion, adding more only gave *carte blanche* to unelected rule makers, who lacked accountability, to dream up madcap but draconian rules and – when such legislation was tested -

suddenly be discovered to have no responsibility. But the rules kept being made and the armies of legislators and administrators and the watchers and the spies continued to grow and the remedies were no better or not cost-effective in any financial or moral sense – and certainly not a response to actual risk. Also, he knew, ninety-nine per cent of the legislation was aimed at soft targets; those that could not resist silly impositions, that is, individuals, while the serious, heavy duty, risks were placed in the 'too difficult' tray and ignored by those whose remit it was to address them. No, Black considered his work rather to be about stopping those who offended society and endangered people in basic *criminal* ways.

He had established early on that beyond the ignorance of many companies lay the hard liners, for which the acquisition of money was far more important than the laying waste of large tracts of land saturated with chemicals, or the danger to health of those who breathed or otherwise came into contact with such substances. It all added up to money versus safety and in these depressed times, survival versus safety.

And some local authorities were due some of the blame, given that they had conflicting priorities, too. Too often they were amenable to the wants of producing companies whose operations were keeping the community alive than listening to those who saw the short cuts and flouting of safety controls as a long term threat to life which more than cancelled out the short term benefits companies could promise.

Such problems were well out of the scope of Black's brief. He had established the truth of the matter many times but it had only been a symptom of the worst aspect of his task; that even successful companies were flouting safety laws. Some, multi-national in size, shopped around for companies in countries that could most easily manufacture otherwise illegal substances with least risk of discovery. His primary task was to seek out such premises but, more importantly, the men behind them.

Until an hour ago he had been confident of doing just that. After several weeks on a most complicated case - involving a web of interconnecting companies where several of these were connected to each other by devious means, and all sharing an equally scant regard for legislative control of the chemical production - he had managed to peel back the layers of deceit and other smoke-screens, until he was beginning to get close to the top man.

Now he had a small incident of poisoning by toxic waste to check out - a mere bagatelle in comparison with some of the incidents he had investigated previously. After all, even though an incident involving the poisoning of twenty-three people had taken place, further aggravated by a mischievous telephone call, it did not register on the scale of potential disaster threatened by the existence of the toxic waste 'lakes' which existed in England or the production of known - and banned

- dangerous chemicals around the world. The sooner he discovered the source and, hopefully, the identity of the anonymous caller in this problem, the sooner he could get back to pursuing the big fish.

It said something for his professionalism, borne of many years in the business of security, that he would apply himself with as much dedication to this job as any other.

Although Inspector Davies had quietly introduced him to Appleton as a scientist, the description was not quite correct. He was involved in the science of detection in many disciplines of science, true, but a glance of his paper qualifications would show no trace of formal assessment in any of them. The secret of how he could operate at all given the complexity of his work was in part due to his versatile brain and the contents of the luggage in his room at the inn.

He had left the most remote of the factories until last. So far, he had had no luck whatsoever though he was sceptical when told by all five locations that absolutely no chemicals were missing. He had learned to distrust whole numbers and, in a way, 'nothing' was a whole number. To have given such information with complete certainty - without having to spend at least a full day checking - added to his mistrust and not only of the factories themselves but of the legislation which permitted such off-handedness to official requests.

The road to the last factory on his list was one of those ribbon-like tracks which follow rigorously the existing contours of the landscape. For twenty minutes he climbed steadily upwards around hairpin bends and along switch-backs before the gates of the Garrison Chemical Company came into view.

As usual getting through the gate was no problem due to his having authorisation high enough to make any management team blink but also, and again as usual, he was escorted wherever he went. By-and-by, and after the usual questions had been answered in the usual way he predictably made his way to the dispatch point. Normally he would have been given all the right answers by the foreman present and then left wondering why he ever made such visits in the first place.

But this time there was a difference. At first the foreman couldn't be located. While he and his escort waited Black looked around, taking in the antics of the fork-lift trucks as they ferried forty-five gallon drums around in something reminiscent of a waltz. It was then that Black got a mild surprise for he had seen the driver of one of the fork-lifts before, chatting in the bar of the *George*.

Then Black checked his impulse to make anything of it. Surely there was nothing untoward in what he saw, fork-lift truck drivers went into public houses just like anybody else. Besides, he had no opportunity then to continue such a train of thought as a man wearing street clothes walked hastily towards them.

'Waiting to see me?' asked the newcomer, who occasionally buried his nose into the handkerchief carried in his right hand.

'Yes,' answered Black's escort, and his tone intimated that he hadn't realised the foreman was away.

'Sorry if you've been waiting long,' he sniffed, unable to get the handkerchief to his nose this time as he was removing his coat. 'I had to get into town to see my doctor. The nurse knew about it. I should have thought she'd have told you.'

'No,' replied the escort, shaking his head. 'But never mind that for the moment. This is Mr Black...' Quickly he introduced the investigator and told him why he was there.

Black watched the foreman closely during this. The man was about thirty-five with sandy coloured hair that was fast diminishing in quantity. His face was heavy-jowled which matched with his heavy build and, when the white handkerchief wasn't hiding his features. Black saw that his complexion was ruddy and his eyes blue.

But it wasn't his appearance that interested Black. Instead it was the foreman's apparent inability to keep still. If he wasn't blowing his nose or adjusting the perfectly neat identity badge, which bore the name Henshaw, he was stamping around the makeshift office and doing this and that to charts on the wall. Given good reason, which he didn't possess, Black would have said the man was nervous.

Henshaw gave all the usual answers. No, he knew of nothing missing. No, there had been no spills, which might have left sufficient residue to be recoverable. His answers, Black noted, came easily enough and at such times his sniffling improved considerably. Because of this the investigator decided to put him under slight pressure and began repeating the questions as if he didn't believe the answers given to them previously. The foreman's response was different now. His answers were still the same but he took more time between answering them and it was back to the handkerchief again.

Although the results of his little experiment were interesting they didn't prove anything beyond the fact that the foreman, had a come-and-go cold. He decided, when the slight pressure on Henshaw had arrived at its peak, to pursue another line of enquiry.

'Are you a local?'

'I live locally in Wicklees. Yes.'

'So you'll know anyone involved in conservation around here then.'

'Conservation? You mean looking after the countryside and all that?'

Black nodded.

'Don't know if I do.'

'How long have you lived here?'

'All my life. Worked here getting on twenty year.'

'And you don't even know things that I know after only being here for a matter of hours?' said Black, accusingly. 'I ask you again: who do you know who is involved with conservation?'

Again the foreman forgot he had a cold as he concentrated on the question. He was nervous and he wanted the man to stop asking him questions. 'Well, Lord Alland speaks out about pollution of the countryside, occasionally. He's the squire around here. Come to think about it he's always on about the damage we're causing to the land.'

'Who is causing?'

'Well, us: the factories.'

Black tried to get a bit more information out of the man but with no success so he left, his escort in tow. He was certain his visit there had been as big a waste of time as that spent on the other sites. He would have changed his mind had he been able to witness the foreman's actions, which took place once Black was out of sight.

For some moments Henshaw stared after the two men. Then he called over the fork-lift driver Black had seen. 'You absolutely sure none of batch 780/7 is missing?' he asked.

The other man looked back resignedly. 'I've told you once. No. The inaccuracies in the records were just mistakes in measurement.'

The foreman continued to stare at the door through which Black had just left. 'Still......'

'Still nothing,' completed the other man. 'Anyway, the records are now changed, aren't they? No problem.'

The foreman nodded and the other man walked off.

In the office the man looked down at the handkerchief wrapped in his right hand and winced. He was still deep in thought and no longer seemed to be suffering from the symptoms of cold. But he still found difficulty in keeping still for he was naturally of a nervous disposition and the events of late had gone a long way to instilling panic within him. With a shaking left hand he reached for the telephone on his desk.

When the person at the other end had identified himself the foreman spoke. He told of Black's visit, interspersing his account with entreaties and accusations. He was almost sobbing when he replaced the phone, such was his state of turmoil, but it wasn't long before his attention was distracted by the pain in his hand. Carefully he removed the handkerchief, which brought with it a mixture of dry and wet blood. Then he looked at his hand and saw the long ugly gash whose puckered edges ran almost exactly the same route as the natural folding line of the palm.

Chapter Four

The *George Inn* had awakened from its afternoon nap by the time Black arrived back at a quarter past six. Signs of life were in evidence around the corridors and stairs as he first visited his room and then strode into the 'rustic' restaurant.

It was too early yet for the main source of dining room trade, that would occur in a rush nearer to nine. For now the room was empty except for the waitress who showed him to a table. Black reflected that the landlord was not slow in introducing his staff to wider aspect of hotel life as the waitress was none other than the girl he had seen earlier.

For the next half-an-hour he concentrated his attention on three main topics: enjoying the food, which didn't require much as he was hungry; throwing surreptitious glances at the waitress who was busy fussing around the tables, and; deciding where he went now in his inquiries after meeting with a dead end at the factories.

It was the latter point that demanded most from his thought processes while the girl drew most ocular attention. For some time the two fought for total control of his faculties and it wasn't until the dessert course, at which point his decision to interview the parents of the poisoned children - which coincided with the girl's disappearance behind a screen - that thoughtful reflection won. Then he heard the tinkle of a phone being lifted off its hook and heard the girl speak.

Curiosity being his strong point, his hearing system zeroed in on her conversation and he would have been interested to learn what was being said but he was not to get the opportunity. At the same instant he heard a commotion at the restaurant entrance and turned to see a crowd of weirdly dressed young men wander in and then over to some tables in front of him.

For a minute or two he listened in on the babble of noise that accompanied their arrival but beyond learning they were involved with a pop-concert in the area, Black's interest stretched no further. However, it had put paid to any hope of listening to the girl and so he returned to considering his own plans.

Behind the screen, which hid the telephone from those in the restaurant, the girl was deeply involved in conversation. Black would have been a little more than just interested had he heard what was said for what was said referred almost entirely to him. Once or twice she rebelled against the instructions of the other person but eventually agreed, being by now in very nearly the same emotional state of mind. As she replaced the telephone she spent a moment or two composing herself before she came out from behind the screen, walked out of the restaurant, and headed for the stairs. As all her movements were out of Black's field of vision he didn't notice her going. In any case the laughter and general level of noise from the group in the corner still had a blanketing effect on all his senses other than the one intent on thought.

Presently he became thirsty and looked around for the waitress in order to ask for a drink. It was then that he realised she was nowhere to be seen and, furthermore, her absence was causing unrest among the group. Occasionally one or other of the louder members would shout out but with no response. Then there was movement from an alcove near the screen where various drinks machines stood and where presumably the door to the kitchens was located.

This movement materialized into the figure of another waitress, a short severe looking woman who carried a cloth covered tray. At her appearance there was a cheer from the group. It was short-lived however as she turned to them and addressed them in sharp tones, saying, 'I do not wait on table.' Then with no more ado she strode to the entrance and disappeared towards the stairs.

It now seemed to Black that the only place he was likely to quench his thirst in the near future was the Bar and so he rose from the table and made for the door, happy to be rid of the group's noisy antics. He had got no further than the corridor however before he slowed his pace. Ahead of him, almost blocking his route were three people, two uniformed policemen and a middle-aged woman wearing a cleaner's overall. He had seen the two policemen before, they being the ones who had accompanied Inspector Davies to the inn that afternoon and subsequently spent time in the Bar. As he approached, one of them nodded, and neither made any protest when he stayed to listen to what the woman was saying.

'I was cleaning, see, and I heard this noise in the dining room.'

'You mean the restaurant,' said the policeman who had nodded to Black.

'That's right, the restaurant,' she confirmed.' I'd just finished cleaning in there and I thought something might have fallen. So I went there to find out what was going on.'

She paused then as a drenched figure squeezed past them and headed for the Bar. Black looked back the way the figure had come and saw through the glass of the main entrance inner-door that it was raining again, the large drops bouncing off the tarmac of the car-park.

'Well I got the fright of my life,' the woman was saying. 'No sooner had I stepped through the door than I heard this crash of breaking glass and the sound of shuffling. Oh, it all happened so fast.'

'Did you see anybody?' This from the by now established as spokesman of the police duo.

'I saw the figure of a man, short hair and that, but beyond that I couldn't say. See, it all happened so fast. I don't move as quickly as I used to and I was still in the doorway when the figure pushes me out of the way and dashes past me.'

'Did you see where he went?'

The woman shook her head. 'I was too busy thinking about getting up off the floor.'

The policeman sighed. 'All right love, let's have a look at the damage.'

'There's not much to look at,' she said, her expression becoming upset. 'I cleared all the mess away.'

She had turned to face the restaurant before speaking but stopped when she realised the effect her remark had had on the policemen. She knew the next question perfectly well and waited patiently for him to ask it.

'Now why would you do a thing like that?'

The reply came from behind them. 'Because I told her to,' said the landlord, closing the bar door behind him. Then he walked towards them, his attention directed to the woman. 'And I suppose because you disagreed with my decision, Mary, you called the police.'

The woman's tone was defensive when she spoke. 'Well, a crime had been committed. A break-in. And I got a heck of bruise where he bumped me against the door frame.'

'But I told you why there was no point bothering the police,' continued Appleton, his tone having a slight edge to it. 'You can't describe the man and apart from that broken cover there was no damage or theft. Can't you see it was our own fault for leaving the toilet window open?'

The 'speaking' policeman was concerned at this and both his expression and tone reflected as much when he spoke, 'Wait a minute, George. Mary was right to report this. On its own it might well be an unsolvable crime of breaking and entering but it is possible it ties in with other information we might have at the station,'

With this Appleton's temper rose. 'And what reason have I got to believe that my efforts will be rewarded with the successful solving of this incident? What confidence can I possibly have in the police's efforts when your own statistics show that at least fifty per cent of all break-ins remain unsolved?'

At this both policemen reddened, more from anger than by any feeling of embarrassment at the force's track record. It seemed to Black, therefore, that this was a good time to steer the two sides back to the case in question, 'Has anyone any idea why the intruder should be in the restaurant?'

Appleton would have glared at him for his own intrusion but he remembered his impression of the man before him. 'No idea,' he responded, icily. 'The till was empty and there was nothing of value apart from the cutlery - and none of that is missing. Nothing.'

'Just the damage to a. . . cover.'

'Yes,' confirmed Appleton, 'just the glass dome which covers the squash machine. He must have knocked it over when Mary disturbed him.'

With that Black excused himself, leaving the unsaid but strongly felt arguments to gain expression in his absence. He had a few unsocial calls to make and time was getting on. Another glance at the pelting rain convinced him of the need for a raincoat and so he went up the stairs two at a time towards his room.

As he reached the half-landing he remembered that he had left the restaurant to get a drink and realised his thirst was now gone. Perhaps meeting the trio in the corridor had taken his mind off such a need. It had certainly caught his interest and he decided to keep the break-in firmly in mind and follow it up as soon as he had time.

A few steps short of his floor he moved to one side to allow the figure above him to get past. At that stage it was just a blur. Then he stopped and looked up and saw it was the girl, who pointedly ignored his nod of recognition as she slinked down the stairs.

'Jolly breed of people around here,' thought Black, dismissing the cold shouldering he had just received, and carried on up to his room.

Within seconds he was on his way out again, shrugging on his raincoat. But at the door he paused to look over his room, a habit he had long had, verifying its neatness. It was as well he did so for he noticed the cases were no longer as neatly arranged as he had left them earlier. Now the nearest one slanted away from the others and the left hand catch wasn't fully secured.

Then he thought of the girl and wondered if she had been in his room all the while she had been absent from the restaurant. He also remembered that it had been she who had connected the call for him when he had first arrived at the inn, a fact he had established by comparing the voice of the girl when in the restaurant to that he had heard by telephone. At first he had put the eavesdropping down to plain curiosity, of course, but if she had been searching in his room the situation was more sinister.

A cursory search of his belongings took all of five minutes but it established that nothing was missing. So theft wasn't the motive for her visit, assuming that it was indeed the girl who had tampered with his luggage. Pensively, he left the room, locking the door behind him. On his way out of the inn he failed to do the proper thing and put his key on the numbered hook behind the desk. He knew he couldn't stop someone getting into his room but at least it wouldn't be by his key.

Chapter Five

By half-past seven of that dreadful evening Black was beginning to believe this was one of *those* days. He had driven and squelched around the shiny streets of Wicklees since just after seven and each of the addresses he had tried had produced absolutely nothing of value to him.

Only five addresses had been given to him by Davies, those of the children's parents his men hadn't yet found time to interview. But he found that Davies hadn't missed anything in leaving these. Their accounts of everything concerning their children in the hours before the incident had even included what they had eaten for breakfast; providing for him the only surprise of the series of interviews, that of the variety and combinations of 'breakfast' foods consumed.

As Black sat in his car and stared out at the rain he knew he was fast losing motivation. Both his visits to the factories and the parents had failed to yield one solitary clue as to how the drum had arrived in the river or who had made a malicious telephone call coincidentally with the incident.

Or was he quite so bereft of direction? Suddenly Black broke out of his staring and started the car. A brief glance at the large scale map of Wicklees was all he needed to pinpoint Highfields Hall. Then he reversed in the narrow street in order to point the car towards the imposing residence of Lord Alland.

The long gravelled drive, which cut through the trees past the lodge, emerged into a large clearing where it ran in a circle in front of the main house and the outbuildings beyond. It was now dusk and Black decided that this together with the driving rain were sufficient justification for him parking as close to the main entrance as possible. It may have been this impertinence that brought someone to the door even before he had rung the bell.

Butlers aren't dressed as they used to be. Nor do they tend to exist under that title except in the most conservative of establishments. But it seems no matter how you change the name of something or dress it up to look different the essential quality will remain the same. Such was the case with the man who confronted Black at the main entrance of Highfields Hall.

Black assessed his age as late fifties although the man had singularly failed to heed the fact. His silver hair was styled as slickly as that of the most youthful middle-aged politician and the craggy face below was suntanned with that peculiar tint produced through patient use of a sunlamp. And his attire of slacks and open-neck trim-fit shirt - with the gold chain and locket at the throat - were as out of place as the glint of intelligence in the blue eyes.

'Lord Alland is not receiving any visitors,' he intoned, with the door kept only partly ajar. 'You must come back tomorrow or ring for an appointment.'

'I don't have the time. Please ask his lordship if he could change his mind and see me.' With that he produced a card.

The man appeared not to be impressed by this gesture. 'Good-night' he said, without glancing at it, and began to close the door, his left hand firmly on its leading edge.

Suddenly irritated by this, Black dropped the card and fastened an iron hand on the one closing the door. For a moment he just held it there, increasing the pressure. It didn't take long for the other man to show his discomfort and while he held the man there, he spoke. 'I told you I hadn't the time. I certainly haven't the time to argue with you. It seems I must ask him myself.'

Judging the man had had enough he pushed on the door, releasing his grip simultaneously. Then, as the door swung open, the other man slipped backwards, almost losing his balance. But if Black believed all resistance to be squashed he was mistaken. No sooner had he walked through the opening than the man lunged at him.

Given a few years back the man's haymaker would have connected with Black's jaw but time had slowed him down quite a lot and his swinging arm merely provided Black with a handy lever to bring his attacker under control.

'Ok, Jeeves, settle down,' encouraged Black, applying strong pressure to the arm he had forced up the man's back. 'We'll get on better if you do as you're told. Understand?' The man nodded his silvery head twice at this and in response Black released him. 'Now let's go and see your boss.'

Lord Alland was slouched in a dimpled chesterfield armchair with his features mainly shadowed due to the positioning of the reading lamp above the chair. On a table by his side stood a bottle of tablets and a glass containing a little transparent fluid.

'Are you quite happy now?' Asked the butler when Black's spoken attempts at rousing Lord Alland had failed. 'I told you he wasn't to be disturbed.'

Black picked up the bottle. 'What are these?'

'A mild sedative. Tonight he took double the dose.'

'Why? And why take sedatives here instead of in his bedroom where he would be much more comfortable?'

The butler's anger was back again now. 'Look, just who are you? What gives you the right to force your way in here at this time of night and ask questions?'

'If you'd read the card I offered you you'd have found out,' replied Black. 'As it is, your tone tells me the pain in your arm is wearing off. If you don't want a repeat, answer the question.'

As if to remember the pain the butler's shoulder gave an involuntary twitch. It didn't completely mollify his attitude but went some way towards doing so. 'Look, I work here. If his lordship wishes to take twice the normal dose of sleeping draught then I can't stop him. Nor can I tell him where to take it.'

'Then tell me why he took it.'

The butler shrugged. 'Pretty obvious, if you ask me.'

'I am asking,' said Black, his voice pitched a little higher in volume than the semi-whispers they had previously been using. At the noise Lord Alland stirred briefly, muttering unintelligibly, but then lapsed back into unconsciousness.

The butler shrugged. 'Because he felt what happened today more closely than most people. It took place on his land and, as squire around here he felt responsible in a way.'

'How so?'

It was the butler's turn to raise his voice. 'I don't know. He tends not to share his inner thoughts with me. Perhaps he felt that he should've kept a closer watch over what was happening on his land and so avoid what happened.'

There seemed nothing Black could do to break through to the facts behind the incident. The man who might have explained quite a bit of what was happening was out for the count in front of him. He would indeed need to return later as the butler had suggested.

In his frustration he looked wildly about him, taking in the rows of books, gallery of family portraits above them and the desk with its expensive ornaments arranged neatly around the desk-pad. Nothing. He could see nothing that could help.

'I'll be back,' he said, and left.

As Black now saw it there was just one more task to carry out before he counted this day as a complete write-off. Therefore when he had parked his car in the *George* car-park he didn't immediately turn in the direction of the main entrance. Instead he took the route he had taken on first arriving there in the afternoon and walked between the side of the inn and the copse of bushes. The rain had subsided somewhat by now, having turned into a light drizzle.

At the rear, gathered in a compound outside the kitchens, and dimly illuminated by light from one of the windows, he found the dustbins. Mary had told them that she had cleared away the broken glass of the break-in. It was this that Black wanted to locate.

After some time he began to berate himself for not having brought his torch from the car as the level of illumination was so meagre as to have him plunging his gloved hands into all manner of rubbish. But eventually he came across a dustbin, which rattled when he moved it, and he soon found a piece of characteristically curved though otherwise shattered glass to which was stuck all manner of dust.

With that he rose from his stooped position and replaced the dustbin lid. Carefully he wrapped the shard in his handkerchief and placed it in his raincoat pocket. Then, as he turned to leave, he heard a noise.

It was an odd sort of noise, unlike any of the occasionally-raised voices or clatter of glasses he could hear coming from the inn. It came from a different direction too, from the cluster of bushes to the side of the building. But although Black noted the fact he had heard something unusual from that direction he gave no outward sign of it. Instead he just returned to the front of the inn by the same route.

At the front of the inn he continued past the main entrance and walked on, veering to the left in a sweeping circle which eventually brought him to the copse but on the side furthest from the light. Very carefully he watched for movement, his night sight becoming more and more accustomed to the limited visibility. Then he very carefully began to move forward through the trees.

Within seconds he saw the man. His outline was only just discernable against the same dim lighting Black had used to search the dustbins. But what gave the man's presence away was the cigarette as, at each inhalation, the weed glowed bright red and Black could smell the smoke.

At that point Black hesitated. Why was the man stood out there at all? And why was he smoking a cigarette; a dead giveaway if he intended that his presence should be unobserved? These thoughts were fleeting question-marks in Black's brain. The answer to them was immediately in front of him so why bother with conjecture when he could just as easily discover the truth from the man.

It was then that he pounced. The figure had little hope of escape as Black's powerful arms were locked around the man's windpipe. A minor struggle did ensue between the two mainly because, on the slight gradient, Black hadn't been able to splay his legs as defence against a backward kick. The man had been very quick to use this ploy, in a jumble of others, which added up to panic, but the result had come as expected and Black had temporarily released his hold when he felt the jab of a heel in his left shin. At this the man had struggled free but his freedom was short-lived as Black hit him with a mighty rabbit punch to the neck, which had the man collapsing to the ground like a marionette without strings.

All that Black should have needed to do now was wait but unfortunately he wasn't given the time. Had he spent more time before coming to blows with the man in thinking things out he might have concluded the watcher was either incompetent, hence the cigarette, or had seen what there was to be seen and was merely waiting there for someone.

As it was the sudden loss of control on his part due to the application of something none too soft but heavy to the back of his head proved the latter case. However, it said something for the bad visibility or Black's thick skull that the blow was not well aimed and of sufficient force to cause Black loss of consciousness. And he soon proved as much by hammering into his assailant.

The new man was larger and hence more powerful than the one Black had first encountered. Nevertheless, Black's superior technique, ungentlemanly, but the product of many years of professional warfare, began to show. He was at the point when the man might sue for negotiation on the question of whether his right arm should or should not remain attached to his body when the other man intervened. He was smaller than the other man but he played even dirtier than Black. Had it not been for Black's sighting of him just in time he would have been dead. As it was he felt the sharp pain as the knife slid along the skin of his ribs.

Then suddenly he was alone. He heard the rustle of leaves and heavy breathing as the two men stumbled to make their escape but his main concentration was on staying conscious. The pain was pretty bad but he found that it eased when he pressed his hand over the spot. He had no idea just how-serious the injury was either and so when he got to his feet it was with some care to say the least.

With his other injuries, mainly bruises and a gash to his shin where the first man had kicked him, Black was not feeling too good. It was with great pain that he took the few paces to the main entrance but found that things got better as he went on. By the time he got to the door of his room he was feeling a lot better and the wooziness of his brain was clearing. Thankfully, the foyer and stairs had been devoid of life when he had stumbled through, which meant no-one had seen the state he was in. Not that there was much to see, beyond traces of mud and the red hole in his raincoat; the latter he hid with his hand. His face was unmarked for, like the two men, he had avoided aiming any punches at the head as, in the dark, he might just as well have tried swatting a fly.

It was as he was feeling in his pockets for the door-key that he heard another odd sound. And it had come from within his room.

There had been very few times in Black's life when he had actually seen red through anger. Now was such a time. That the two men should not only have presumably left him for dead but then raided his room too, well, that showed lack of respect for the professional he was. It was time he taught them a lesson. It was also rage that sent him in there without thinking.

The light was off as he pushed back the door but he caught sight of the figure hardly discernible in the shadows, stood against the wall. It must have been desperation that sent him straight at the figure, striking out with a fist that had all two-hundred pounds behind it. If the fist had arrived on target with the momentum and force intended then a charge of manslaughter would undoubtedly have followed. As it was, he had forgotten the group of cases in the way, or the bed beyond them and so, even before he had reached the figure, some fifty per cent of the force had been absorbed by his falling over the obstacles in his path. That this caused him to fall was the reason why another twenty-five per cent of the force disappeared from the blow. Nevertheless, his fist did connect and he heard the figure slump to the floor at just about the time he was burying his nose in the bed-clothes.

Then, realising his utter folly, he waited for the other of the two men to bring the earth down on top of him. He had given up. He didn't deserve a chance at all. He had begun to treat this whole day as a waste of time and his consequent loss of concentration had meant he had reaped the cost of his mistakes. Or would shortly, he knew.

But nothing happened for all of five seconds and so he gingerly pulled himself up from the bed and switched on the light. Then he groaned at what he saw in the corner. There had been no second man in the room because there had been no first man. The figure in the corner had long blonde hair and wore a dishevelled waitress uniform that was too tight for her.

Bringing the girl round was not a pleasant business as it was attended by groans and tears as well as some slight convulsions. The faces she pulled in her distress were enough to frighten away anyone who didn't feel entirely responsible for her predicament. And Black certainly felt embarrassment and shame at causing such injury to a woman. So much so that by the time she was at the point of having only a very bad headache - suitably dosed with aspirin - he had almost forgotten that it was she who had brought it all on herself by being in his room unannounced.

'You all right now?' he asked at length, adding this to the less intelligible reassurances he had offered as she was regaining consciousness.

I suppose he expected a brave smile followed by an 'I think so' from the girl. He was to be disappointed. What he did receive was a long look at her beautiful hazel eyes. They were glaring at him.

'How do you think I feel after being violently attacked and knocked to the floor unconscious?' she cried. Then she winced as she remembered the pain in her head.

For a moment Black was taken aback at the unexpected reply. And also, despite the harshness in her words, the cultivated voice she possessed. 'Perhaps you'd feel better if I took you down to the police station where you could translate your feelings into a charge.'

'That would suit me just fine.'

'Good,' said Black, getting up from his kneeling position on the bed. 'We'd both have something to do. For me, I could make out a charge of burglary.' Then he paused. 'No, wait a minute, make that attempted murder.'

'Attempted what?' the girl cried, incredulous.

'You had a knife in your hand when I lifted you onto the bed.

'I was scared, I wanted to protect myself.'

Black breathed in noisily through his teeth. 'Still looks like attempted murder to me. And of course my knocking you unconscious was an act of self-defence.'

He winced then as he thought of what the charge might have been had the full force of his blow contacted with the girl's frail jaw. He winced too as he felt the resumption of pain in his chest, which the excitement had temporarily blotted out.

The girl's glare was a little more subdued now and Black was of the mind to extinguish it. 'Perhaps now you will tell me just what you were doing in my room.'

The speed of her response demonstrated that she had been ready for the question. 'I work here. I was checking the heating in your room.'

'And the light? Do you normally stand in wait in the dark with a paper-knife in your hand?'

'The light went out.'

'I see. The light went out so you reached for the nearest weapon in order to defend yourself.'

'Yes.'

'Then I believe the best place for us really is the police station. Would you come along with me or do you want them to send a car?'

His words upset the girl's confidence. 'The police station? Why? I've just told you what happened.'

'And a lousy story it makes, too. You said the light went off. I won't argue with the obvious. But you switched it off! I know because it was in the up position before I switched it on to see who I had knocked unconscious.'

'So I switched it off,' she said, offhandedly. 'I thought you might wonder why I was in your room. I panicked.'

'Don't forget the knife.'

'The knife?'

'You were on the far side of the bed when I arrived which meant you most probably heard my coming. As the paper knife was on the dressing-table by the door you had to have scooped it up on your way. Not the panic movement of one worried about the unseemliness of being in a gentleman's room after dark, is it?'

'Less of the gentleman.'

'The choice is yours,'

'Definitely not a gentleman. There, I've decided. My jaw still aches abominably and as for my head...'

'The choice is between the police station or telling me the true story of why you were in my room,' he persisted.

There was silence for a few moments. Black watched the girl closely. She didn't seem to be frightened at all, more fed up at having to endure this episode. Then he got to wondering what a well-spoken, well-coiffured girl was doing serving time as a waitress. Not that she was too neatly attired or composed at the moment. She looked as if she'd been dragged through a hedge backwards.

The expensive watch she wore added another question for it was probably worth several weeks of a waitress's wages.

'All right, Mr Black,' she said finally.

'Knows my name, too. What's yours?'

'Rose... Oh, what's the point? My name is Katherine.

'I've heard the name before. Police Gazette, perhaps?'

Katherine Ross sighed. 'All right, funny man, cut out the games. I'll just give you the story.'

'Go on, I'm listening,' encouraged Black, gingerly folding his frame into the armchair and trying to hide the discomfort this caused him.

The girl saw it in his face this time, and her own expression softened a little. 'Are you in pain? You've gone a bit pale.'

'Never mind. Get on with the story.' he whispered. 'And please? I know your uniform is a little tight but please try-to cover your thighs.'

The girl dragged the crumpled fabric a millimetre lower, a difficult operation while laying half slumped on a bed. Then she smiled, none too pleasantly. 'I thought you were just ill, not ill-mannered, too.'

Beyond just listening to the girl's story Black learned that Katherine Ross was a pretty smart person. Her story was of how an amateur detective had decided to keep tabs on the man whose presence threatened that of her boss. He learned also that here was a girl who had spirit and determination and who at the same time was capable of great compassion. It wasn't only the content of her words which gave him this impression, he also read between the lines. Presently, and against his better judgement, he began to admire the person who animatedly spoke to him from the bed.

'Let me get this straight before you go on,' he interrupted. 'Your parents were killed in a plane crash when you were nine and Lord Alland took you in as one of his own.'

'That's right. My mother was Lord Alland's sister.'

And you stayed with him after you had finished university to become his personal assistant.'

'You're so quick, Mr Black.'

'Thank you for the sarcasm, I'm sure,' he replied.' And by the way my first name is David.'

'Noted, Mr Black.'

Black ignored the barb. 'You say Lord Alland was a father to you.'

'He still is - a very good father.' For the first time Black noticed a fleeting softness in her expression.

'And you were keeping tabs on me to protect him.'

The girl's eyes grew sombre. 'He was in a terrible state when I saw him this morning. He had just heard of the incident here and he looked as if he wanted to die. It took me an hour to get it out of him. Even now I don't understand what he was saying. I've never seen him so upset - or even anything like it.'

'What did he tell you?' prompted Black, worried that she might never get around to telling him.

'He said there had been this awful mix-up. He - and some others - had wanted to draw attention to the pollution which was taking place around here. They wanted to become a group of informants of what was going on without being wrapped-up in the public lime-light of a pressure group. It was as if they wanted to give the authorities time to put their house in order without the need to make national headlines about it.'

At this she smiled softly. 'So gentlemanly, really. So like Uncle Timmie.'

'Who?'

The girl didn't at first understand. Then she said, 'Uncle Timmie. Lord Alland. His real name is Timothy Melhuish.'

'Sorry, carry on.'

'Well, it seems they arranged for some men to plant a drum containing a very weak mixture of one of the chemicals known to be produced illegally in the area. I can't remember if he told me what it was. I was a bit upset too, you see. I'd never seen him in such a state.'

'Yes,' said Black, noncommittally. 'Who were the men who planted the stuff?'

'He didn't say, but I got the idea that they got someone to arrange it all so that they wouldn't be involved.'

'You mean a third party?'

'I think so. A member of the Circle - that was the name Uncle Timmie gave to the group - was chosen to do all the dealings with the men who planted the drum.'

'This Circle had no intention of causing the incident which followed?'

'None whatsoever. He was adamant about this. He said they just meant to call the authorities, drawing their attention to pollution of some river.'

'The River Breck,' put in Black. 'The Area Health Authority received a message relayed to them by a newspaper man. The journalist received an anonymous telephone call at precisely the time the children were floundering in the river out there.'

Noting the edge to Black's voice as he mentioned the children Katherine's voice became raised. 'I've told you that he had no intention that anyone should be poisoned.'

'How could they be certain?'

'I don't know. I asked him the same question but he said that he knew someone who had assured him on the subject.'

'Why didn't he tell all he knew to the police?'

'He was going to. I even rang them myself but he changed his mind. He would only agree to me coming into town. When I left he was in a pretty sorry state.'

Black thought about this and now knew why Lord Alland had taken the sedative.

'And what about approaching the media. Doesn't that conflict with their policy of making quiet overtures to polluters rather than appealing to the national press?'

'I don't know. Perhaps this was a worse case than usual. Perhaps they had failed to heed the normal warnings.' She buried her face in her hands. Then, her voice muffled by the hands, she spoke again with indecision very much in evidence. 'I don't know. All I do know is that I love Uncle Timmie and I'll do all I can to help him.'

For a few moments there was silence.

'Why did you take to watching me?' he asked.

The girl dropped her arms, her eyes red and wet. 'Because I heard Mr Appleton mention you were a scientist here to investigate the incident. I decided that you would be close to whatever was happening about it and so I thought I would stay close to you.'

'And that is why you paid two visits to my room apart from listening in on my telephone call this afternoon.'

At first the girl was tempted to bluff it out but it was obvious from the start that it was a waste of time. Instead she simply said, 'Yes.'

'You telephoned any information you had to Lord Alland.'

Again the girl paused before answering. 'Yes.'

Black thought for a moment. 'You contend that your Uncle had no knowledge of how a dangerous chemical came to be in that drum or that poisoning of the children was intended.'

'Yes I do?' she cried. 'I'm absolutely positive that he knew nothing of what happened and that the blame rests squarely with the men employed to dump the drum.'

'So you believe that as far as Lord Alland is concerned the drum incident is all over.'

' All over,' she confirmed. Then her eyes lit up in a sign of hopefulness. 'What will you do?'

'Have a bath,' he replied, innocently.

The girl's pent-up emotions exploded at that. 'We're talking about people's lives and reputations and all you can do is announce you'll have a bath?'

'Personally I don't give a damn about people's reputations. It's up to them to take care of that, not me. But I am worried a lot about people's lives - the children's and others - and I will do my best for them. But this isn't as small a game as you would like to believe, Miss Ross.' He pulled back one side of his raincoat. 'And if I'm to help at all I had better establish in just what state of health I am. A bath will help me decide.'

With that, Black got to his feet and in so doing obscured the large area of blood revealed as he had pulled the raincoat to one side a moment earlier. The girl stayed where she was for a second longer, still looking at the spot where Black had been seated. Then she seemed to come out of a trance.

'Oh, my God,' she cried, swinging her legs off the bed. 'Who did that to you?'

'A couple of unfriendly types, who decided to play this game too close to my chest.'

'That isn't even funny.'

'You're telling me!'

'I'd better get a doctor.'

'No doctor,' instructed Black. 'But you might like to rustle up a bandage or two.'

'There are some in the medical box downstairs,' she responded, and made her way somewhat shakily to the door.

She hadn't made it that far when the telephone rang and Black answered it. As she leaned on the wall she listened to his terse responses then looked at him questioningly as he replaced the receiver.

'All over, you say?' he asked.

The girl's frown was all the response he got to this so he added, 'That was my temporary boss. He thought I'd like to know that someone just phoned without giving a name. The caller invited his attention to the fact that a full drum of the same chemical found in the River Breck exists and what does he think about that.'

The girl's expression was scared. 'It couldn't be Uncle Timmie who called...'

'I know that too,' interrupted Black. 'You see I saw him only just over an hour ago and he was sedated to the gills. There is no way he will be making phone calls until at least tomorrow. Now, how about those bandages?'

It took a few seconds more for the frown to disappear but then she seemed to pull herself together and left the room.

Chapter Six

Black had almost completed a tedious one-handed shower by the time he heard the sounds of her return. He had soon discovered the wound was not as bad as the splash of blood on his shirt had suggested and what he now saw in the bathroom mirror was a long, neat and barely bleeding incision which, to his relief, was not deep enough to show the whiteness of rib-bone beneath.

'What took you so long?' he called through the bathroom door.

'A bit low on gratitude, aren't we?' she countered, her breath laboured. 'I had to get the key from the landlord.'

'Did you say who the stuff was for?'

'I just said it was for one of the male residents.'

Black opened the bathroom door. 'You might just as well have well told him my name. When I sneaked a look at the register this afternoon I noticed I was the only person registered.'

'I didn't realise you were desperate to keep it secret,' she replied. 'But you're wrong you know. There's a rather eccentric old lady staying here too.' The words came mechanically as her attention was directed at Black's dripping torso, wrapped as it was in a towel covering only the area from waist to knee. His right palm was laid flat against his chest as he applied pressure to the wound to staunch the bleeding.

'Don't go all coy on me, Miss Ross,' he said.

'I wasn't,' she responded whip-like. 'I just thought it would have been better for you to use the towel to get dry before you left the bathroom.'

'A touch difficult with one hand.'

'Oh, I see.' She fiddled with the box she had brought with her. 'Well let's get both hands back into action again.'

The possibilities offered by her words passed through his mind in a flash bringing a smile to his lips, which the girl saw. 'This may not be major surgery I'm about to carry out but it could be quite painful all the same,' she warned.

At this Black adopted a more sombre expression and the girl began to first dry and then apply a dressing to the cut, which she all but encapsulated in a mass of adhesive tape.

'I see. Spinning it out, are we?' said Black.

'How do you mean?'

'Leaving me to the torment of imagining all that sticky tape being ripped off later.'

'It just means that you won't rip it open should you try anything energetic,' she answered, and this time Black felt an odd tingle run down his back. 'But seriously,' she continued, 'you need stitches in that...'

'I've got to check in with the hospital sometime and see how the children are doing,' he interrupted. 'I'll have them look at this and the other thing at the same time.'

'The other thing?'

Black pointed to a spot at the back of his neck. 'Where they hit me.' Then he pulled a face and swung his head from side to side. 'All the muscles seem to have bunched in a knot.'

The girl's curiosity and concern had her jumping to her feet and moving around Black to take a closer look at his neck, 'No mark that I can see,' she announced, 'It's probably just tension and not an injury at all,'

'Perhaps you could give it a rub.'

The girl's hands, which had been prodding around the skin at the base of his neck, leapt away at his words as if they had received an electric shock. Then she quietly put them back, gently massaging the muscles beneath the brown skin. 'The things you get yourself into, Katherine Ross,' she announced resignedly. But inside she was secretly thrilled, feeling all kinds of sensations where there hadn't been any for some time.

'You're doing a grand job, nurse,' he said after a while. 'Now about this other pain I have down...'

The rest was lost in the girl's giggles as she pushed him off his already precarious perch on the side of the bed and watched him tumble to the floor. But when he slid to the floor the towel fell away.

It was at that moment that they both stopped dead in their emotional tracks. Although Black unselfconsciously replaced the towel the incident had been a show-stopper and they both knew that they were not far enough along the emotional track to accept this as an introduction to what was in the back of their minds.

However their senses were now at a peak and there seemed no way they would dissipate. It might have been embarrassing but it turned out not to be, as Black depressurised the situation with a quip about someone having to wear the pants around here, at which point he disappeared into the bathroom with his clothes, augmented by a clean, blood-free, shirt.

When he emerged fully dressed their emotions were back on an even keel. The girl had tidied up the bits and pieces of the medical kit and returned them. Nothing was said about what had happened and both felt this was the best course of action.

'What was that you were saying about an old lady staying here?' asked Black as he replaced the suitcase and began opening another.

'The other resident, you mean?' responded the girl gaily, relieved to have a point of conversation well clear of the one she feared. 'It's just that she's a bit of an eccentric as far as I can make out. Never leaves the inn. Has all her meals sent up.'

Black wasn't really interested in the girl's response but his query had got them talking again and that was necessary as he had some important questions to ask her.

As they spoke he began to open the customised luggage, bringing various items of electrical gadgets from the made-to-measure padding. Such was the girl's interest in what he was doing that she didn't notice the way the conversation was going until suddenly she felt the pressure on her.

'Look I've told you all I know,' she said a little irately.

'Impossible.'

'Why so, Mr Black?'

'David,' he prompted, at the same time picking up his bags. 'Because I find it impossible that a personal secretary could to know so little as you pretend to know about her boss's activities.'

It was only the grunt that followed his words, as he remembered the pain in his chest, that stalled the anger she felt. Instead, she said, 'Here, let me help,' and she picked up one of the bags.

'Thanks,' he said, as she placed it on the dressing table. 'Look, he didn't decide on his method of operation in anti-pollution and then put it into operation without conversations and planning with the members of this Circle. That is surely obvious.'

'What's in this?' she asked, pointing at the bag she had just lifted onto the dressing table.

'A computer,' he answered, quickly. 'Don't avoid the question.' Then, when she didn't say anything, he added, 'Well?'

'I've already told you all I know.'

For a moment the girl stood still, looking at the computer. Then Black gently put the fingertips of his right hand under her chin and turned her face towards his. 'There may be things you have forgotten to tell me because they didn't seem important, Miss Ross.'

'Katherine,' she uttered.

Black smiled briefly. 'Katherine,' he acknowledged, 'we need to go over your story again. All right?'

The girl tried to nod.

'And while we're at it,' he continued, removing his hand, 'we'll apply a cold compress to that bruise on your jaw.'

'Yes, Dr Jekyll,' she said as he moved to the bathroom. 'What sort of information do you need?'

'Mr Hyde was the bad one,' he reminded her, going into the bathroom.

'I must be warming to you,' she responded.

Black smiled and dipped a corner of the towel under the cold water tap, speaking over his shoulder at the same time. 'Information? Oh, I'm not completely sure. But how about his appointments book? Perhaps a name recurs quite often that you can't account for as being a part of normal business. That would help.'

Then Black returned and gave the compress to the girl. She was stood at the mirror fingering the swollen area of her chin. 'What a beauty,' he said.

She gave him a wan smile then. 'For a moment I could have believed you weren't just commenting on the bruise.'

Black's response was lightning fast: 'Bruise?'

The girl smile again and moved away quietly, her expression thoughtful.

'You understand what I mean,' said Black after her, his tone back to being business-like. When she didn't answer he said it again.

'I've been thinking,' she announced. 'No personal assistant worth their salt would need to consult an appointment book to come up with the information you want. And I am no exception.'

At this she turned around and picked up the telephone directory on the table.

'What are you looking for?' he asked.

The girl looked up. 'A name springs to mind that fits with what you were wanting. The name is Holland and he's something to do with Garrison.'

'The Garrison Chemical Company?'

'Yes, that's right. How did you know?'

'I toured all the factories this afternoon,' said Black. 'What's significant about this Holland?'

'Just that Lord Alland saw him a couple of times in private and even wrote to him. I never did discover why.'

'Describe him,' urged Black.

'It's a bit vague. He was such a nondescript man, really. I think he had sandy or reddish hair and was quite a stout person.'

'You're sure it wasn't Henshaw...'

The girl's eyes lit up. 'Henshaw, that was it!' Then her expression changed to puzzlement. 'Now why did I think it was Holland?'

But Black wasn't really listening. He was putting the pieces of a jigsaw together in his mind, linking what he had just been told to what Henshaw had said. The foreman had spoken of Alland, too. Perhaps he looked upon Alland as a protector, the name automatically springing to his lips when Black had begun to pressure him at the factory.

'Do you know where this Henshaw lives?'

'I'm trying to find out,' she replied, rifling through the directory.

'Make sure you get the telephone number as well,' he instructed, his manner now urgent. 'If I'm right in my thinking he could be our link with the people who caused the incident. He might even be one of them.'

The girl looked up. 'I don't follow.'

'Just keep looking,' he urged. 'It's quite simple, if it's true. Henshaw was Lord Alland's go-between. The man was a bundle of nerves when I saw him. With good reason too, I shouldn't wonder. If he is the only link with the villains then he's the only one who can point the finger at them.'

'You're not suggesting he's in danger.'

'Precisely that. Have you got the details?'

She proffered the scrap of paper she had written on but he didn't take it. Instead he picked up the telephone receiver and offered it to her. 'It had better be you who calls him. He knows you and may take your advice as someone close to Lord Alland.'

The girl took the instrument. 'What do I say?'

'Just that he is to stay where he is and we'll be out to see him in a few minutes.'

'Why don't we just go round?'

Black sighed, impatient. 'We don't know if he's there, yet. And if he isn't we're no closer. If he is then he might be tempted to run. Your voice might convince him to stay.'

Henshaw was at home when she called and Black's theory was proved correct for he promised to stay there until the two arrived. Soon afterwards Black and Katherine Ross were speeding their way over in Black's car.

'It's true, you do drive too fast,' she said as he screamed around a corner.

'Who told you that?'

'I forget. Someone who came in the bar this evening and was talking to the landlord. Please slow down.'

Immediately Black eased off the accelerator. 'Sorry. Force of habit. I always seem to be in a hurry.'

Then he looked over and saw that she was still tense. 'About Lord Alland,' he began.

'What about him?'

'Is he married?'

'Oh yes,' she replied, interested. 'Nice person, too. Although Lady Alland isn't in the best of health.'

'What's wrong?'

'I don't really know. She's never really been well as far as I can remember. She's away on one of her rest cures at the moment.'

'Isn't that a bit odd.'

'How do you mean?'

'Well, that she isn't by her husband's side during his troubles.'

'You don't understand Lord Alland. That's the last thing he would want. Any commotion would be bad for her health.'

'That bad.'

'I'm afraid so,' she confirmed. Then she sat upright, her eyes pressed close to the windscreen. 'I think this is the place. Yes it is. Green Lane.'

Black stopped the car outside a small semi-detached house whose ground floor windows were illuminated from within. As they walked up the short path the girl checked the door number just visible against the one she had committed to memory. 'This is the one,' she announced.

Several times Black pushed the bell, hearing the muted chimes on each occasion. But two minutes after their arrival they were still outside the front door and there was no sign of anyone from within coming to open it. The door had no handle, it being of the common type that required a key - and only a key - to gain entrance.

'Let's take a look around the back,' said Black.

'He could have popped out for a moment,' suggested the girl trying to find a reason for the situation.

Black came to a halt at the rear door that the light from the room behind it clearly showed was slightly ajar.

'Or he ran for it after he spoke to us,' he mused aloud. He was beginning to regret having phoned and not accepting the girl's suggestion of calling round without warning.

'Door's open,' he announced. 'Let's take a look round.'

As they crossed the threshold Black became aware of a tightening of the girl's grip on his arm.

The first room they passed through was the kitchen. A small dining room adjoined this while a corridor led from the kitchen to the front door with just the lounge to the right and the stairs to the left. Unlike the other doors he had so far seen inside, the lounge door was shut. On sighting this Black paused, urging the girl to move back down the hall. Then when he was squarely facing the door he opened it and pushed it back.

Immediately, the girl screamed.

For a moment or two Black could see no reason for her reaction as apart from signs of a struggle there was nothing for even the squeamish to worry about. Then he realised his field of view was different from that of the girl and he moved round to see what had been visible before she had turned in a defensive move to shield her sight.

Henshaw hadn't run away. He had stopped answering doors too, along with just about everything that a live human being does. Henshaw was quite dead. Black saw a knife wound in the man's chest, at the same spot as his own, except that it was obviously much deeper.

Having made sure there was no-one else in the house Black led the shocked girl to the kitchen and then rang the police. As they waited for them to arrive Black coached the girl in what she was to say as he felt there was no point in divulging all they knew until he was ready. Then he went for a second look at the body.

He noticed a cut on the palm of the right hand and concluded that Henshaw must have grabbed for the killer's knife hand and found himself holding the blade instead.

Beyond that Black was disappointed with the lack of clues. There seemed nothing else of significance, either in the man's pockets or the room itself, so he broadened the search to include the other rooms. The result of this was just so much wasted effort although he did find something, which interested him, in the hall.

A raincoat hanging from one of the hooks was mainly dry but there was the odd damp patch here and there. This prompted much thought on Black's part and gradually he came to the conclusion that not only had someone's raincoat been on top of the one still hanging there - and one soaked through from the downpours of the day - such an occurrence suggested the killer was known to the dead man.

Then he felt in the raincoat pockets and found a blood-stained handkerchief. Perhaps he was wrong and there had been no struggle at all. That might well be the case if the man knew Henshaw and could pick his moment to kill him. And that meant that the cut could have been caused by some other means. He went back into the room where Henshaw lay and looked again at the hand.

It was difficult for him to say, but it seemed the wound was older than that in the chest. At which moment, Black remembered the man and his 'come and go' sniffing. A blind to cover the injury to his hand? It would need more thought, he knew, but he already had other thoughts pressing on this; other pieces of the jigsaw coming closer-together if not actually fitting.

Black then returned to the kitchen and the girl. 'How did he sound on the telephone, Katherine?' he asked gently.

The girl was still upset and her answer was subdued in tone. 'Guarded, I think.'

'Did you get the impression he had anyone with him?'

The girl looked up. 'He kept his voice low.'

Black held her hand. 'That's all I needed to know.'

The conversation on their way back to the inn was naturally subdued, the girl feeling the shock of seeing Henshaw's body quite keenly. But she had stood up well to the onslaught of police questions and stuck to giving the answers as Black had instructed. Black had fended off Inspector Davies's questions without much trouble, telling him that the reason for their presence was just that they were calling on the merely to confirm what was and was not produced at the factory.

Davies had accepted that but was a little sceptical as to why the girl should be there. This had been a more difficult ball to field especially as at least two of the policemen in Davies's force had seen Katherine at the inn. It only required for one of the several waiting outside the house to come in and recognized her as Rose when Davies understood her name to be as declared in her driving licence and more questions would follow. The result would not be disastrous but Black had kept ahead in the past by telling only what was necessary at the time.

As it was, the moment came and went smoothly without Davies pressing the point. In part this was due to Black's intimation that he and the girl were more than just friends. Shortly afterwards they had left.

'I think I ought to go back to Highfields,' said the girl as they approached the *George.*

'That wouldn't be very wise at the moment.' said Black. 'You've now learned that the stakes are high enough to kill for and though I don't exactly know what the stakes are, I know your safety is in jeopardy.'

The girl swung round in her seat to look at him, her eyes wide. 'My safety? Why?'

'I see you're getting back on balance again. You're questioning everything I say,' he put in quickly before getting around to answering her question. 'Why your safety? Because if the killer was in the room with Henshaw when you phoned he will know you are involved in some way.'

Just then Black slowed the car to a halt in the *George* car-park and switched off the engine. Then he turned to face the girl. 'He may not know just how much you are involved but that assumes he doesn't know you. If Henshaw said who he was talking to and the killer knows you then he must realise you are a danger because you know all the people who came into contact with Lord Alland.'

'Thanks for cheering me up.'

Black smiled gently in the semi-darkness. 'You've got to know the facts, Katherine.'

'So what do I do?'

'You stay here, at the inn. With me,' he answered. 'You don't go anywhere without my knowledge until this whole thing is cleared up.'

The girl touched his arm. 'You don't have to look after me, David.'

'But I want to,' he insisted. 'And even if I didn't want to, I have to. It was at my suggestion you made the call and therefore my fault you're in this predicament.'

She tried to object but he pressed the point. 'Look, one telephone call and I could make this official. Besides, you can help me. You have local knowledge and we might even jog your memory some more about the Circle.'

'You win, but what about my job here?'

'When are you next on?'

'Tomorrow evening. In the dining room.'

'Then we've until tomorrow evening to think of something,' he decided. 'Now are we going to stay out here all night?'

Katherine shrugged her shoulders. 'You're the boss.' she said, and Black was gratified to find her shock at seeing Henshaw lying dead was fast wearing off.

It was just after half-past nine when they arrived at his room, having called briefly for some things from hers. Then Black retrieved a laptop computer from one of his locked bags switched it on. Placing it on the dressing table, he briefly glanced up to use the passkey for the Wi-Fi, before he was head-down again.

Katherine looked on. 'Is there anything I can do?' she asked then, feeling at a loose end.

Black spoke over his shoulder, hardly pausing in his typing. 'Not at the moment, thank you. I have some research I have to check through.'

'I'll take a long bath then,' she responded tired-ly. 'It seems to have been quite a day.'

'Excellent,' came his response. 'Then perhaps you'll be able to get an early night.'

While the bath was running Katherine looked at her face in the mirror. The bruise hadn't discol-oured as much as she had imagined it would but the swelling was there and it was tender to the touch. She didn't confine herself to study of this but took in her whole image managing to see most of her reflection in the large wall mirror.

She was now twenty-seven years old but as she looked at her figure she was convinced it was as trim and firm as it ever had been. It wasn't that she looked at herself everyday: she tended to casual observation of her figure preferring merely to check for change.

Similarly she worried little about her looks. She was a career girl who met a lot of people in her work as Lord Alland's PA and she had to look presentable. She tended to use only the merest hint of make-up and her hair was of a style that required little maintenance. The rest of her acclaimed beauty she attributed to good bone-structure.

Her sudden critical appraisal in the bathroom mirror caught her by surprise. Why did she look so closely now? She still pondered this and vainly tried to ignore the obvious answer as she turned off the taps and got into the bath. Then she lay back and closed her eyes. In the quiet void left by the rushing water from the taps she heard the clicking of the keyboard as Black 'talked' to the computer.

For a few moments the girl felt the heaviness of relaxation come over her as the warm water soothed the tensions away. Many thoughts passed through her mind and once her eyes opened as she remembered the sight of poor Henshaw lying on the floor. Then she began to doze and seconds later was asleep.

Half-an-hour had passed before she awoke, the change in water temperature being the cause as it had now cooled somewhat. She felt cool though not cold but noticed that the goose-pimples had risen on her breasts, the nipples standing firm. Reluctantly she returned to full consciousness, blinking her eyes several times and stretching in the restricted space. Then she sighed and lay still while her ears picked up the clicking of the keyboard once more.

An odd smile came to her lips then. 'He works too hard,' she thought. Then her smile became almost a grin until she realised what she was doing and stopped. Slowly she emerged from the bath and began to dry herself very carefully.

The keyboard noise ceased long before she left the bathroom and when she finally stepped through the door it was to see him still sat at the dressing table rubbing his eyes. 'You can overdo it you know,' she warned.

Black turned slowly, reaching a hand behind his neck to massage that area, 'You didn't go down the plug-hole, then?'

'Not quite.'

Black looked at the towelled girl and the bundle of clothes she carried before her, 'You can change over there,' he said. 'Promise I won't look.' With that he turned back to the screen and began tapping the keyboard again.

Then his eyes lighted with surprise. Behind him the girl had put her hands on his shoulders close to the neck and was massaging the area he had complained of earlier. For a moment or two he simply enjoyed this without any other sensation until he became aware of the faint scent she wore and he felt a surge of excitement well inside him. And then he knew neither would be satisfied with a simple massage.

He turned swiftly, rising at the same time to draw Katherine to him and look down into her very serious expression. His hands held her arms, gently at first then with an increasing pressure as he felt her weight shift. Then he kissed her hard, and was barely aware of her clinging to him before that daze ensued, which wrapped them into a warm cocoon divorced from reality, and which took them almost unconsciously to the nearest bed.

Chapter Seven

It was half-past ten, when the buzz of the telephone shocked them from the slumber into which they had so recently fallen. As Katherine struggled to a sitting position, Black was already speaking into the instrument. Then, even before she had begun to realise what was going on, he had replaced the receiver and was leaping out of bed.

'Who was it?' she asked, now waking up fast.

'Hospital,' he responded. 'And you'd better get dressed pretty quickly. I said we'd be there in ten minutes.'

At this she too left the bed, but at a somewhat slower pace than Black. She was aware now that there were disadvantages as well as advantages to having his protection, and the need to go wherever he went was very much one of them. For a moment she was tempted to say as much but bit on her tongue instead. Then she went over to him and held him, halting his progress in getting dressed.

After the first kiss he gently but firmly pushed her away. 'Don't burden me with conflicting priorities. You might win,' he growled.

At this she giggled and began sorting out the bundle of clothes she had dropped to the floor on leaving the bathroom. 'Did they say what it was about?'

'Didn't want to say over the telephone. That's why we're going round.' He looked across at the girl then, noting that she had dressed very quickly and was now opening the door to the corridor. 'Now where are you going?'

'I won't be a minute,' she replied. 'I think I might need a little make-up on this bruise. We don't want people to think you beat me, do we?'

Black noted that she waited for his agreement, standing immobile in the doorway. He knew he couldn't protect her out of his sight and wondered: what if someone was waiting in her room. He should go with her but he needed to close down the computer, which was still whirring away - but that took time. Then he came to a decision. He would take the risk. 'Two minutes, no more,' he instructed.

'Yes, sir,' she responded and left with a shake of her long blonde hair.

They didn't quite make the deadline Black had promised on the telephone. It was almost that before Black cautiously called at the girl's room and with mixed feelings found she was still doing repairs to her face.

His expression was quite serious as he said, 'Do you always spend so much time on your make-up?'

Katherine saw the look he gave her but her reply was given smilingly. 'Only when I've been knocked out by the man I am trying to impress,' she said.

At this Black's serious expression cracked and he smiled back at her. 'Come on,' he said, playfully dragging her away from the mirror, 'we're late.'

'We've just had our first death,' said the man who had introduced himself as Doctor Fisher, paediatrician in charge of the incident children. He tapped his chest: 'A weak heart, which hadn't been previously diagnosed.'

Katherine Ross's face was white. 'Who was it?'

The doctor had a board under his arm and he almost took it out but then changed his mind. He knew the details off pat, he had been worrying over the child's health for some hours before she died. 'Shirley Dent. Seven years old.'

'Tragedy,' uttered Black, unable to find words to describe his feelings properly.

'Yes, it is that,' confirmed Fisher. 'And murder.'

'Murder?' cried Black and in the otherwise empty ante-room the word echoed dully of the walls.

'All right, let's be technical and call it manslaughter,' responded Fisher. 'Admittedly the killer couldn't have known the poor child had a bad heart but in my book it ranks as nothing short of murder.'

Black's incomprehension showed on his face. 'Wait a moment,' he said, his brow etched in a deep frown. 'I'm as against industrial pollution as the next man but let's keep this in perspective.'

'Oh, I'm doing that, Mr Black. I am not being overly emotional, either. You've yet to know why I called you over.'

'I thought the child's death...'

'Very important, of course,' interrupted Fisher, 'but I could just as well have given you the bad news over the phone. No, I asked you here to introduce you to something that a colleague of mine has found - and to hear what he then told me.' He moved them towards the door. 'I'll leave you to make up your own mind.'

The lights were dim in the laboratory, to which Fisher escorted Black and the girl. For a moment, Black thought the place deserted until he saw a slight movement from near a desk in the far corner. Then they saw a white-coated figure remove a pair of spectacles and rise to meet them.

'Doctor Holland, I presume?' said the girl before Fisher could introduce them.

There was a flicker of surprise in the man's eyes but he recovered quickly. 'Mr Holland, actually. My world is biochemistry.' He peered closely at the girl. 'And you, my girl, are Katherine Ross, Lord Alland's secretary.'

The girl nodded and looked meaningfully to Black.

'Have you told them anything?' said Holland to Fisher.

'Nothing.'

Holland glanced at his watch. 'We won't wait. I will come straight to the point and tell you that the chemical analysed as coming from the container in the river was not the causative agent in the poisoning incident. Certainly, traces of 2,4,5-T were found in every patient but of such insignificant amounts as to be discounted as having any effect on their well-being.'

'But it was something in the river?' asked Black.

'Presumably so, yet I don't understand how or why,' he said his expression reflecting some undisclosed mental anguish. 'It's a nightmare.'

Black felt he needed to nudge Holland. 'What was the causative agent?'

Holland raised his head. 'Ascorbic acid,' he said, his tone incredulous. 'Plain old aspirin!'

He was not alone in finding his words incredible. Katherine Ross was so unbelieving as to ask if he was sure.

'Absolutely positive,' returned Holland. 'The tests and the symptoms both corroborate the conclusion that each patient swallowed the equivalent of four or five tablets.'

'Surely such a dose could kill a small child,' said the girl, her face still pale.

'It might have if we hadn't got some of the stuff out of them.' It was Fisher who answered her and his tone was bitter. 'Have you ever given a stomach pump to a small child? Not something for the emotionally squeamish.'

'Are you saying there was a high concentration of ascorbic acid in the river water, too?' put in Black, addressing himself to Holland.

'That's the odd thing. Not even trace concentrations of it were found in the analysis carried out after the incident. Yet pinpointing any other source isn't easy: checking who took what and when and deciding what substance the poisoned people took, which was specific to them only... Well, we're still checking the permutations. Analysis of the stomach contents is still going on but we're still awaiting results.'

Black thought about this for a moment before speaking again, at the same time plunging his hand into the raincoat pocket. 'Could the taste of such a concentration of aspirin have been masked by, say, orange juice?'

'Certainly. But what are you getting at?' replied Holland.

Black pulled a handkerchief from his pocket and unfolded it, revealing the shard of glass which was still grimy from its time in the dustbin. 'If you find ascorbic acid on that I will be able to tell you for certain how the drug was introduced to the children.'

'What is it?' asked Holland.

'A piece of a glass dispenser that once contained orange juice.'

'Where did you find it?'

Black would have answered Holland's question but Fisher's mind was obviously unable to process his private thoughts silently for he forestalled the answer with a question of his own. 'Why do a terrible thing like this?' he asked, heatedly. 'Who could willingly cause such suffering to children?'

Black wanted to know this answer too and for a moment his curiosity vied for expression with his answer to Holland's question: curiosity won because he remembered the girl's earlier reference to the biochemist. He decided to play a long shot. 'Yes, why would anyone want to do such a thing. Mr Holland? You are a member of the Circle. Perhaps you can tell us.'

The question certainly got a reaction for immediately Holland's face dropped. Then he swung round on Fisher. 'I thought you had told them nothing.'

'I didn't. I left it for you to repeat what you told me,' answered Fisher indignantly.

For a moment all was quiet. Black could hear footfalls elsewhere in the hospital and the screech of a swing door being pushed open but his concentration was on Holland. Then Holland sighed. 'I was going to tell you anyway. I asked Fisher here to call you for that purpose. My conscience should be clear at the moment but it isn't. I only know that our plan seems not only to have misfired but to have been taken over and modified by someone else.'

In the next few minutes he added a few more pieces of the jig-saw to those Black already knew. He told mainly the same story Katherine Ross had recounted, except he added a lot of detail. It was true they had begun social blackmail by demonstrating to polluters they had information on their operations, which would be released to the world media if such operations did not immediately cease.

Holland didn't know how many Circle members there were. He knew only of Lord Alland and one other, Henshaw, and the latter he had only learned about by accident. He said he didn't know of all Lord Alland's operations either, but believed behind all the small dealings they were engaged in he sensed there was one big operation that had preoccupied him for some months. Moreover, he suspected the dumping in the Breck had been part of this larger campaign to bring the offenders to their senses. He revealed that Holland might never have learned anything at all of Alland's activities had it not been for Holland's approach to him as a man he could trust with information on an aspect of pollution he had uncovered himself.

'You're saying then that Lord Alland didn't always keep you fully in the picture.'

'Exactly,' replied Holland. 'We always knew what form the protest would take but not always who it was against.'

'But you knew what was supposed to have happened with the River Breck dumping.'

Holland nodded.

'What was the planning behind it?'

'Lord Alland said that he knew someone at a factory who could obtain a small quantity of a certain chemical that was being illegally produced in vast quantities. The idea was that this man would get the substance and then alone approach other men he knew to dump it in the River Breck. Then Lord Alland would call the Area Health Authority, drawing their attention to the existence of this substance and have them call a crash audit of all the factories in the area.'

'Was this one of your more extreme operations?'

Holland nodded vigorously. 'The most extreme. Normally we would just send the assembled information to the culprits telling them of copies we had in our possession. That usually did the trick. But for some reason Lord Alland wasn't convinced this would achieve the required results in this case.'

'Any idea why?'

'None.' Then Holland paused. 'It could be he wanted people to start asking questions. A more public approach, but short of banners and things in Trafalgar Square.'

'Go on.'

'It was a stroke of luck that the man he had got to obtain the substance knew a third party to deploy it. That way we wouldn't be directly connected.'

'So no-one but Lord Alland's go-between knew the people who actually deployed the drum?'

'Not as far as I know.'

Black sighed and inwardly thought of the frightened wretch he had interviewed earlier in the day. Then he looked at Holland again. Here was another frightened wretch but for another reason. Black thought he knew why but he asked the question all the same. 'What was your part in this?'

Holland's shoulders sagged. 'It was my job to ensure that a non-toxic dose was used. Or at least an amount that would have no harmful effect on anything with which it came into contact.'

'Well, we know that the substance in the drum wasn't responsible for the poisoning,' reasoned Black.

'Yes, but even so the amount of 2,4,5-T released into the river was far higher than that which I specified. Apparently all sorts of wild-life died in the vicinity of the drum.'

Holland's voice had become tense so that each word had begun to rise higher in tone. If Black had ideas that this man's complicity was any greater than he had said he now discounted them. Embattled by fears and guilt and unable to understand what was happening Holland was dangerously close to cracking. As Black's formative conclusions weren't quite ripe he couldn't console the man with the factual answers his scientific brain required.

'And that was your total plan? Nothing to do with this incident?'

'I swear it,' said Holland gravely, the recollection of the suffering very evident in his eyes. 'I can only think that these people have other motives and wanted us to believe that the drugging was due to the chemical in the river and by so doing discredit Lord Alland when - as now - all is revealed.'

'Then you are convinced Lord Alland is not involved beyond what you have indicated.'

'Absolutely positive,' he said.

'And so am I,' said a voice from behind them.

All four of them turned to peer into the gloom at the words. Then the figure approached, the shoes clicking on the tiled floor. It was the Chairman of Wicklees Council.

'Good evening, one and all,' he said as he entered the pool of light that illuminated the others. 'Sorry I took so long but I came as soon as I got your message, Fisher. What a dreadful business this is turning into.'

Holland spoke then, his tone respectful. 'I was just telling them...' He got no further because the Chairman waved a long-fingered hand dismissively. 'I think I got most of it, Holland. You see I paused by the door rather than interrupt the conversation before I needed to. At this point he seemed to notice the girl for the first time and gave her a salutary nod, recognition in his eyes. As an associate of Lord Alland, he would have seen the girl on a number of occasions.

'What is that?' he asked, indicating the shard of glass on Holland's desk.

'A piece of an orange container I found in the dustbin behind the George Inn,' replied Black.

'What is its significance?'

'We have yet to discover that, but I believe it fits in well with something I have been thinking about. I can tell you more if Mr Holland can discover if it bears traces of ascorbic acid.' With that he turned to look quizzically at the Chairman, for he had emphasised his last two words.

The Chairman got Black's meaning. 'Yes, jolly old aspirin. I heard that, too. But come along Black, you must tell us of your theories. What is your interpretation of the events we have so recently witnessed?'

'We're witnessing a take-over,' responded Black. 'However misty a veil seems to cover this incident we do know that a take-over is taking place. It started, of course, with Lord Alland's merry band, and intentions that I can hardly call criminal. Its actions I might frown upon but intentions, no. They set up an incident that was apparently aimed at nudging a polluter to mend his ways. It involved the procurement of a chemical in a very-small amount and, because they were apprehensive of being lumped with pressure groups on discovery, they chose to have someone else dump the chemical. Those are the bare details as we all know them.'

Black paused then to look around the four other people. There was a heavy silence now as each concentrated on his words, not even the far off sounds of the hospital intruding now. 'The go-between and *procurer* of the chemical was Henshaw. Only he knew the people who deployed the drum.'

'Henshaw,' said Holland. 'Yes, that makes sense.'

'So he is involved with these people,' mused the Chairman.

'Was,' put in the girl in a voice hardly audible.

'Was?' asked the Chairman. 'What do you mean?'

'She means he's dead. Murdered this evening.' Black's tone was level and flat.

For a few moments no-one said anything. Then Holland broke the silence. 'God, it's incredible. How did he die?'

Black told him.

'Do we assume that he fell out with the people who did this dreadful thing?' asked the girl.

'It's the best theory I have at the moment.'

'Do you believe he was involved in their part of the plan?' asked the Chairman.

'No, I don't think so in the way you seem to mean,' responded Black. 'He respected Lord Alland too much to turn against him in such a fashion. It was he who procured the chemical and I feel sure it would have been the full extent of his participation had things gone to plan.'

Guessing greater meaning in Black's words than was immediately evident, the Chairman looked pointedly at the investigator, 'You mean he was involved more deeply than that?'

'Yes, but only in an attempt to stop it.' Black was tired now. It had been a long day already. He felt he wasn't making the greatest sense in trying to treat Henshaw with the respect he deserved by stating the facts in their entirety. 'Somehow he got wind of what had really happened at the children's picnic. His first reaction was panic and he tried to remove the evidence. He broke into the George Inn this afternoon in an attempt to wash the orange container which, I believe, had contained a high concentration of ascorbic acid. Unfortunately, a cleaner surprised him and he dropped the container, smashing it into a number of pieces and cutting his hand in the process. However, he managed to escape undetected.

'By the time he returned to his works he was in a right old state and needed to grip a handkerchief to staunch the flow of blood from his palm. I know because I saw him when he got there whereupon he tried to disguise the injury by making out he had a severe cold, which necessitated the constant presence of a handkerchief.'

'Poor man,' commented the girl.

'Word of this must have got back to whoever 'they' are and they obviously didn't trust him in his excited state. They must have believed he might go to the police at any time and now he had gone and drawn attention to an incident in the *George* only hours after the poisoning. Whatever their reasoning with regard to this they decided to keep an eye on the dustbins where the glass had been deposited.'

'How do you know all this?' asked the Chairman.

'Because I decided there was something odd about the break-in and was proved right when I met a reception committee just after picking up that piece of glass,' he pointed to the object on the desk. 'In the struggle that followed I received a superficial knife wound upon which Miss Ross here later practiced first aid. Which reminds me, I must call on your casualty department.'

The other pairs of eyes traversed to take in the girl but their minds were obviously elsewhere as their expressions didn't seem to take in her presence. 'Later, when I had grounds to suspect Henshaw's involvement in all this I had Miss Ross call him and tell him to expect a visit from us. At the time he was not alone and I believe he was trying to persuade whoever was with him to stop whatever was planned. I'm sorry to be so vague but it cannot be helped.'

He then went on to tell them of their visit to Henshaw's house. When he had finished there was a moment's pause before the Chairman spoke. 'And you say the knife wound was in the same position as the one suffered by you?'

Black nodded.

'What in heaven's name can we do?' asked Holland.

'Henshaw's death is being investigated by the police and no doubt they are going to ask a lot of questions about the incident now that the little girl has died,' said Black, finding himself the unelect-

113

ed leader. 'We must offer every assistance to them while at the same time pursuing our own inquiries.'

For a moment or two Black waited for input from the others but no-one spoke, seemingly content to let him go on.

'As for these inquiries of ours, we've been told that a full drum of this chemical 2,4,5-T exists,' he continued. 'We must await the auditor's report to discover from which factories it could have come. I know that Henshaw got a little from Garrison but that doesn't mean that the rest came from there.'

'There's not enough missing,' said Holland, his look quizzical.

'What? From any factory? How do you know?'

Holland looked from the Chairman to Black. 'The report was in a couple of hours ago.' He turned then and picked up a document off his desk. 'Here it is. Of all the factories audited not one has even a litre of 2,4,5-T that isn't accounted for.'

Black's expression was not benevolent when he directed his gaze at the Chairman. 'The report has been out for hours and you couldn't get a copy to me?' he asked, his voice raised.

'The report is inconclusive,' dismissed the Chairman. 'There was no point in getting it to you before the morning.'

'Then let us do another audit!' Black's tone was one the Chairman had never had used in conversations with him but then the investigator was never too worried at the noises he made, just actions and results.

The Chairman said nothing, however, and Black continued. 'There has got to be stuff missing if only to bear out the fact that far more 2,4,5-T was released into the river than Mr Holland prescribed. No five minute audit will prove anything. Only a full twenty-four hour blitz will do.'

The Chairman was obviously a diplomat and it showed when he said without frills that he would arrange for a second, more thorough audit.

'Now these people didn't casually inform us of the existence of a drum of 2,4,5-T without wanting us to become very worried at the applications they might put it to,' continued Black. 'Therefore we must assume they have lower motives than the Circle and would want something a little more concrete than assurances of good conduct in future. In a word, gentlemen, ransom. We must assume they will barter deployment of this stuff against what they want.'

'That's a hell of a lot of 2,4,5-T,' said Holland, then his tone became grave. 'If it is 2,4,5-T.'

'What do you mean by that?' Black's words were icy.

'2,4,5-T produces a bi-product in its manufacture which is infinitely more dangerous. Legislation has banned the most potent strain of this and new processes do not produce it in any quantity. However this is a more expensive process than the old one and it may be possible that someone is using the old process still, in which case they would hardly keep records of the amounts produced.'

'What is it called?'

'TCDD. Trichlorodibenzo-para-dioxin,' he breathed, seemingly in a trance. 'A substance so potent that it's the subject of a world-wide ban. It has no known antidote and...'

'Do you think we could concern ourselves with facts,' said the Chairman, irritation in his voice. 'At the moment we're talking about 2,4,5-T, a drum of which might possibly exist. We're not certain in any case and speculation does nothing but waste time and worry us unduly.'

'Hear, hear,' agreed Black. 'Our objectives while awaiting the result of the second audit must be to pursue the problem of identifying these villains and locating possible target areas for such a substance.'

'And how do you suppose to do that?' asked Fisher. 'You don't even know where to start.'

'Lord Alland,' said Black shortly. 'You may be certain he can have had nothing to do with this but let us accept that he started it all.'

'It is of course your problem,' said the Chairman, 'but you are wasting your time trying to pin this on him. One only has to know the man, of his military record or even that in business, to know that he would never stoop to such villainy. Surely the way he has carried out this campaign against polluters should tell you that.' He shook his head vigorously then. 'No, you are barking up the wrong tree there, Mr Black.'

'Perhaps you have an alternative idea,' proposed Black.

'You could concentrate on the 'where' problem and let the police worry about the 'who' bit.'

'I could,' admitted Black. 'I understand you're loyalty to Lord Alland but I must see him. What I will do is postpone the interview until tomorrow. But in the meantime I will require your clearance for a computer link-up with the police NID computer. I need links with others but I can arrange them myself.'

'I'll do my best,' said the Chairman.

'And I'll need it in an hour.'

The chairman looked surprised at this but nodded.

'I'll brief Inspector Davies in the morning,' continued Black. 'Unless you would like to do it.'

But the Chairman shook his head. 'No, I'll leave it to you. I shall need to pull some strings to get you this link-up.'

Shortly afterwards they split up. Black and the girl going first to the casualty section of the hospital where Black's wound was stitched and dressed.

The Chairman was as good as his word. When Black and the girl returned to the inn there was a message for Black to call a certain number. He recognized the number as the contact number of the National Identity computer and knew that he would feed all his queries through the operator there.

'You know how to operate the switchboard, Katherine,' he said in the deserted foyer, 'could you have incoming calls

ring straight through to my room?'

'You can, indeed,' she replied and moved behind the small reception desk. Then she made three switches on the small panel, and returned to his side. 'There. And I've stopped it ringing down here, too.'

'And a pretty face as well,' he said lightly, patting her on the head.

'It might have been before you had to go and...'

Black clapped a hand over her mouth, his eyes looking wildly around. But when he spoke it was with a smile. 'You're not going to let me forget that in a hurry, are you?'

With his hand still in place her response was muffled 'but Black believed he had the general sense of what she was trying to say. 'I thought so,' he said. Then he released her and they went up to his room.

It was gone midnight now and both of them were feeling tired. However, Black knew it was important that he should begin his computer-aided search for the 'who' and 'where' of the problem as soon as possible. He therefore suggested the girl went to bed and knew from the tiredness he saw in her eyes that there was no danger of her misunderstanding his meaning.

As she did as she was bid he moved back to the computer. Behind him the girl listened for a few moments to the clicking of the keyboard and remembered her thoughts when she had heard this noise several hours before. She also remembered the reasons behind the thoughts and reflected that she had enjoyed the task. Then, knowing there was nothing more she could do, she allowed the tiredness to swamp her and fell into a deep sleep.

Black spent the first hour of the new day feeding in the parameters of his search to various other computer agencies as well as the NID. On the 'who' side of the search his parameters were intended to form a 'ballpark' of possible suspects; radicals, conservationists, known criminals whose methods might be mirrored in what he suspected or what had occurred. The possibilities and assumptions were endless and he even had the facet of who used a knife in the particular fashion he had personally experienced added to the long list. So desperate was he for ideas to narrow the field that he ended by feeding in a list of all the people he had met since arriving in Wicklees.

That had taken the major part of an hour. What took up the rest was the 'where' component. By feeding in the simple parameters of how most profitably to deploy a drum of toxic waste in order to have the greatest leverage he left the remaining computer agencies the task of providing lists. His only addition, which he included to narrow the field by some degree, was to localize it by restricting the operation to an area within a radius of fifty miles.

He knew the first replies couldn't possibly be in straightaway so he looked at the results of his earlier research for the job he had been doing until seconded to the Chairman's employ. There was several month's hard work concentrated in the folders on the computer and he hoped he might find a link between what he had found then and what he was seeing now.

By the end of the second hour of the day he was quite bleary-eyed and aware that he was becoming confused. What decided him to call a temporary halt was the fact that he was beginning to suspect everyone on his list from the landlord of the inn to the Chairman himself! At that point, he briefly prepared the computer for when the first replies came in. Then he moved away from the computer and lay on the bed.

The first of the replies came in seventeen minutes after his head had touched the pillow. It was quite a wrench responding to the call but within five minutes he had completely forgotten the effort it had required. The answers, or rather possibilities, came in thick and fast in the next hour and he couldn't possibly check through all the data immediately. But he latched onto several possibilities which arrived with the first reply, some possible answers dealing with the 'where' side of the problem.

Because of this he literally had to postpone reading the other replies, including the NID computer survey until later, merely having the time to acknowledge the information by email, before continuing with his previous task.

By three-thirty he was sure that what he was seeing on the screen was as hot a lead as it was possible to get. The list of possible targets had been given a value as a guide to confidence in its feasibility. There were several similar targets and Black had to consult a map to begin weeding the less likely possibilities from the list. Then he was left with two. Both were water orientated; one a water treatment station the other a reservoir. Obviously, the search programs had come up with the answer that most damage, and therefore most ransoming power, could be obtained by poisoning the water through these locations. Black's further interpretations got it down to the fact that both served the same water route.

His tiredness was completely forgotten now as he balanced the arguments for and against both sites as targets. It took no more than a few seconds for him to arrive at an answer as he was sure that it was more difficult to get into a water treatment complex than a reservoir. Therefore, he had isolated his best hunch to just one location. He looked at the name; Freshwater Reservoir. 'Let's hope it stays that way,' thought Black.

His work completed for the moment, he made a backup of his work to a USB key storage device, as he always did. He followed this with something he almost never did; he slid the device under his bed. Then he switched off the computer and, after putting it away, he moved over to the girl's bed and gently woke her up.

'What is it?' she asked, her speech blurred.

'Questions, always questions,' responded Black gaily. 'I'm taking you for a drive in the country.'

As he was speaking she looked at her watch on the bedside table. Then her eyes were wide-open. 'At a quarter to four? It's the middle of the night!'

Black laughed. 'It means that if we leave now it will be light by the time we arrive. We could watch the sun rise over the hills.'

The girl moaned. 'Listen, if I sign a note saying I absolve you from all responsibility for my safety, will you let me go back to sleep?'

'Damned ingratitude,' protested Black. 'Offering you a ride out in the country and all you can think of is staying in bed all day.'

'A slight exaggeration, I think,' she riposted. 'But seriously, David, if I'd known that your protection meant I had to follow you around like some kind of lap-dog. Well I'd... Oh, what's the use.' With that she threw back the covers and stumbled from the bed.

'Where are we going to now?'

He told her.

'Do you mind if I take along my wellies?'

Black's mind was obviously elsewhere for her question didn't quite register.

'Your what?'

'My wellies, for the nice country mud and things. They're in my room.'

Black began to reflect on the advantages of the note she had suggested but with an iron will brushed the thought from his mind. 'OK, tell me exactly where they are and I'll get them while you're dressing,' he offered, and he didn't quite manage to hide the note of resignation in his voice.

Chapter Eight

'What I can't understand is why this chemical is on the market at all if it is so dangerous,' said Katherine, breaking the comparative silence that had existed for most of the journey so far.

They were well into the single-track network of the Pennines proper now with Black's promised sunrise failing somewhat by arriving as a thin grey band of light which served only to illuminate the dark brooding clouds filling the rest of the sky.

Her words dragged Black from the reverie that had occupied his mind ever since leaving the inn. He had spent the time thinking over all the aspects of the case during their journey and had almost forgotten she was beside him. But perhaps that wasn't quite correct: she had figured in his overall survey of the situation, if mainly for the reason that he had come to respect her gutsiness in the face of potential danger. He found he had to admire the fact that she didn't reveal any fear for her own safety, a notion supported when he had left her alone for a while prior to making this trip.

More impressive was the way she had gaily wandered off to her room before they went to the hospital. It wasn't every woman, or even man, who could still function normally without any obvious signs of strain when they knew they might share the same fate as had befallen Henshaw. Yes, she was quite a girl, he thought. Or rather stupid.

'The 2,4,5-T you mean?' he responded, shifting his weight in the seat.

He had kept his speed down along the narrow country lanes and not only out of consideration for the girl; such was the zigzag and switch-back quality of their route it was a choice of blowing hot and cold between accelerator and brake or keeping the speed down to a low even pace. Unfortunately the latter caused cramp in Black's leg and his efforts to relieve the pain tended to cause a twitch in his steering which also brought them dangerously close at times to the dry-stone walls which ran along either side.

The girl waved a hand dismissively at his answer. 'Whatever it is called. It just seems stupid to be worried about it being dumped when, as Holland said, it is in general use as a herbicide.'

'That's looking at it from the wrong end of a telescope,' returned Black, quizzically. 'Just because it is in general use does not mean it is safe. As a matter of fact 2,4,5-T has been banned by many countries. Britain was one of them, for a time.'

'For a time? So it has now been proved safe?'

'Some people say so, others say it is still a very-dangerous chemical.'

They were driving up a steep gradient now and Black had to shout above the roar of the engine. 'You see, many people consider the greatest danger from TCP was another ever-present substance within its make-up called dioxin, the TCDD spoken of by Holland,'

'I think I've heard of dioxin before.'

'I would be surprised if you hadn't. Dioxin is just a shorter name for 2,3,7,8-Tetrachlorodibenzo-para-dioxin, otherwise TCDD. It was an ingredient of Agent Orange, the defoliant that wasted large tracts of Vietnam. It was the causative agent in a law-suit whose plaintiffs numbered many thousands, all claiming injurious effects from exposure to Agent Orange,'

As they reached the point in their upward climb where the road swung round to the left in a hair-pin Black paused for a second to concentrate on his driving. Then as the roar of the engine subsided in response to a more gentle climb he continued speaking in a quieter voice. 'They're still battling through the courts several years after they started. With billions of dollars at stake one can hardly blame the producers of the substance from putting up quite a fight. Anyway, TCP, the TCDD-bearing substance, has since been banned extensively throughout the world.'

'Except that It's now back in Britain?'

Black nodded. 'And I hear even the US is bringing it back. I can imagine the uproar that decision will cause.'

'If they can't decide on the safety side of this substance, why don't they just ban this TCP anyway and have done with it?'

Black smiled grimly. 'Because it seems the world can't afford to. If TCP were no more efficient than the many other herbicides on the market it would disappear overnight. Unfortunately it just happens to be far more efficient than even its nearest rival. That is why it is beginning to come back into legal usage. However, there are controls on the content of TCDD in relation to the TCP.'

'You mean although it is now allowed for use here it must have much less of the dioxin present in each batch.'

'That's about it. Other countries have an upper limit of nought point nought three parts per million concentration whereas Britain specifies that it mustn't be above nought point nought one parts per million.'

'Not easy to visualise, is it?'

'No, but the fact is that any concentration of dioxin is harmful. The consensus of opinion is that dioxin should be avoided in any amount. It is some indication of their concern when they have spent the last ten years developing techniques to measure the presence of TCDD to an accuracy of parts per trillion!'

It was marginally lighter now but there was no doubt it was not going to be anything more than a dull day. Presently the car breasted a hill, which allowed them to look down on a wide expanse of water whose furthest extent was shrouded in a low-lying mist. Nearer at hand they could see a long curved line which was the parapet of a dam.

Connected to this by a flimsy catwalk which jutted out at right-angles was a small stone-built structure some distance out in the water.

'Beautiful,' decided the girl.

'It is that,' agreed Black, having to admit that there was something pleasing to the eye in the grey majesty of the scene below. From their vantage the track dipped steeply before it stretched out across the top of the dam and up again into the hills beyond. But there was one feature of the landscape which marred the scene and gave an industrial quality to it. Across the great mass of hill which formed the eastern boundary of the reservoir was gouged a reddish scar of a track which descended in a long drag to meet the road at the causeway.

As they got closer Black could begin to pick out the detail of the scene. Out on the water almost hidden by the mist was a small boat and he could just make out a couple of figures and the attendant devices for fishing. Closer to him and at the water's edge he saw a sign that forbade such activity and supposed that he had found at least one possible reason for the angler's practice of indulging his hobby at unearthly hours.

'How much would they need to dump in this reservoir to cause harm to a person's health?'

Black thought for a moment. 'Impossible to say as I don't know what concentration of TCP will be used. If it was just TCP I should say a few hundred gallons but if it contained a high reading of TCDD then that is a different matter altogether.'

He knew he hadn't answered the question very well but this was in some part due to the sudden realisation that after driving for so long to get to the reservoir he had yet to formulate in his mind just how two people went about searching for a drum of toxic chemical over the vast area they could now see before them. Not only that, he now knew just being at the site provided no indication this reservoir was the target. These conclusions inflicted upon him a sharp jab of mental anguish. It was as if he had only just begun to understand the enormity of the problem facing him; of discovering the target *before* the threatened event took place.

'If it is the new legal formulation of TCP which is to be deployed,' he continued slowly, 'then I should say we have no problem if the amount as reported is only one drum. After all, if this reservoir holds say a million gallons of water and you dump in it fifty gallons of TCP - with a concentration of only nought point nought one per cent of TCDD - then it isn't going to be harmful by the new legal definition. But what if it is the old formulation which has a high proportion of TCDD present?'

'But won't all the old stuff have been dumped by now and only the new stuff be available?'

Black smiled again. 'You mean dumped for some council to lose track of or build housing estates over it, you mean?

'You're quite bitter about all this, aren't you,' she said, a new interest in her gaze.

Black ignored the accusation but responded to her question instead. 'I wish I could believe that all the old stuff was out of circulation by now. Unfortunately the main problem with the new process is that it costs more. Greater control is needed in temperature and pressure throughout the conversion and the yields aren't so great as they were. It all boils down to economics and my fear is that what may be deployed here is newly-made but illegal strength TCP.'

'Oh,' she responded simply.

'That's as good a reaction as any. If this is the case then it's quite possible a drum load will raise the whole of the contents of this reservoir - assuming it is the target - above the safety threshold I told you about. In my opinion your employer – and uncle - was trying to get at the producer of illegal strength TCP.'

Black brought the car to a halt at the start of the causeway that ran the whole length of the dam. From here, he could see the gate in the parapet, which allowed access to the valve-house along the catwalk. Even at a distance of fifty-yards he could see that the gate was almost off its hinges and was in any case unlocked. Also he could see the door to the valve-house, or rather the green-flaked wooden frame set in the heavy stone-block constructions. The door itself was missing. In that one brief glance his overwhelming first impression was of dilapidation through long term neglect.

'What are we looking for?' asked the girl innocently.

If she had known Black's state of mind at that precise moment she doubtless wouldn't have asked the question for he was far less clear of the answer than when he had left the inn. In the end he said, 'I'll tell you that when we find it. But don't expect any hoardings with 'Tourist route to nasty men's toxic waste site' to be scattered around.' Then he opened the door and climbed from the car.

They spent the next half-an-hour splashing around two of the three levels, the lower level being almost completely full of oily water and flotsam. Black studied everything visible in great detail, matching inlet with outlet valves and so forth, and by the end of this period he knew how the simple machinery was meant to operate.

He also discovered that the owner had applied the same effort in stopping unauthorized tampering as he had in keeping people out of the valve-house in the first place. Quite simply he had allowed the machinery to fend for itself against the elements and now Black found he could hardly budge the valves, so rusty were the screw-threads serving them. But criminal though the degree of neglect seemed to him, they found nothing among the debris and stench of the valve-house which could possibly indicate the reservoir was the target.

'Who does this belong to? Any idea?' he asked, as they stepped through the door on their way out.

'I think all this land around here belongs to Uncle Timmie,' said the girl, a frown creasing her brow. 'I've been thinking about this place ever since we got here. He used to take me all over with him and I'm sure this used to supply a mill some way down stream. Did, I should say, because there are no mills still operational around here.'

'Well there is one crime against him for a start.'

'Crime? What do you mean?' she cried, two spots of colour touching her cheeks. 'I've told you. Uncle Timmie is no criminal. He is the sweetest man on earth.'

'Just look around,' suggested Black. 'This place is a death-trap. A few determined men with crowbars could shut off the water outlet from this dam. Give it a few rainy days and a storm and the whole structure could be washed away.'

'But who would do a thing like that? And why is it Uncle Timmie's fault?'

Black shrugged a reply to the first question, he reflected that he was becoming paranoid; suspecting only the worst of everyone now, so desperate had he become to find a lead. 'It's Lord Alland's fault because he hasn't kept this place in good repair. I'll bet he's never had the structure surveyed, surely a most important requirement from time to time if he's to have any guarantee that a million gallons of water won't suddenly burst on an un-suspecting populace in the valleys.'

For a while there was silence. Then when the girl spoke it was with a thoughtful expression on her face. 'You don't like him do you? You think he is more involved in this thing than I've told you. You probable think that I'm...'

She didn't finish because Black turned her around to face him, squeezing her shoulders as he looked down into her eyes. It was his turn to wear a frown. 'Look, I don't know anything, Katherine. I do know that I suspect everyone until I am sure they're clear.' Then he smiled gently. 'If it's any consolation you're not on my list.'

They embraced then, the girl burying her face into his shoulder, and Black reflected that he found lying too easy these days.

From the valve-house they went over to the opposite side of the parapet and gazed down the wide slope at the rush of water some fifty feet below. The water spewed from the outlet duct in a powerful jet several feet in diameter, which then turned rapidly into a swollen mass of foam to swirl noisily down a wide concrete culvert.

Black studied the layout below for several minutes. He could see more than one outlet duct in the grassy slope. There were two more above and to the sides of the one that was feeding water into the culvert at the moment. Black realised that these dry outlets were served by two other valves inside, each labelled with fading tallies bearing the legend: 'Storm Sluice'.

Normally the newer dams had simple storm sluices at the top of the structure but well below the parapet. It was in this way that they compensated for a high water level and thus prevented the dam from being rolled-over by the massive weight of water, which could build up over the parapet during a storm. It was a novel design to have an internal compensating system, he knew, but then a lot of the older dams didn't have one at all!

He then recollected the dim memories of reports he had seen on failures in some older dams where seepage had undermined the clay structure and, in turn, caused failure under 'storm' conditions. He remembered reports of one such failure and the loss of life that had occurred when the great surge of water had gouged a furrow several miles long, destroyed everything in its path. The thought made him look at the level of the water in the reservoir hut although it was high, some ten feet from the level of the road, the very fact that the valve-stems were rusty and a great torrent was leaving the main outlet valve suggested the dam had managed to look after Itself for some time without the need for supervision. Perhaps he had been a little too critical of Lord Alland's maintenance of the dam, but only a little.

Black sighed as he turned away, his eyes still anxious to take in any clue that might convince him that the journey hadn't been a total waste of time. Nothing. Even the small boat had disappeared which, though it didn't surprise him as they probably suspected him to be an official, disappointed him because he had wanted to ask them if they had seen any other activity during their stay.

'Let's go,' he said presently, and began walking the hundred yards back to the car.

It was seven now and it had begun to rain. The droplets were heavy and interspersed with sleet and up in the hills he could see the cloud coming down. 'Back to the drawing board,' he sighed.

The girl noticed his disappointment. 'Still, I got my ride in the country,' she smiled.

But Black didn't reply.

He was still engaged in silent meditation, mainly on the subject of what to do next, as the car climbed to the top of the hill that had been their previous vantage. At the top, the girl turned from looking back at the reservoir which now was almost obliterated from view by the quickly falling mist. In the silence, she studied the barely visible valley before them down which the road zigzagged sharply.

Katherine Ross allowed Black to take the first two bends at high speed in spite of the limited visibility before she decided discretionary consideration of his problems was not sufficient motive for getting oneself killed. 'David, please slow down,' she said.

Then she took in the sweat that was gleaming on his brow and knew that this was no absent-minded speeding on his part. She sensed but hadn't yet put into words what was happening then, but Black said it for her. 'I'd love to, Katherine, but I'm afraid I can't.'

'What is it?'

'Brakes gone,' he answered simply, unable to manage longer speeches as his attention was sorely needed for concentration on avoiding the dry-stone walls to either side of the track.

Frantically he fought with the gearshift trying to select a lower gear as a brake but beyond the high-pitched grating noise attending this move he achieved nothing there, his speed now far too high. Beside him Katherine Ross's breathing was erratic as she took ever frequent breaths at the lightning appearances of walls and the almost impossible angles Black had to deal with in steering the vehicle clear of obstructions.

Soon their increasing speed and ever decreasing visibility began to tell on Black's reactions for he just hadn't the time to assimilate danger and take corrective action and they were now bouncing off the walls quite frequently.

'Cross arms,' he panted. 'Then keep your head back on the restraint.'

A moment later he risked a glance to see if she had done as she was told. Satisfied he spoke again. 'I think there's a broken wall ahead on the left. Going to try running it up the hill.' What he didn't mention was that loose stonework from the broken wall littered the ground around the opening and might cause any kind of damage to the underside of the car.

The girl said nothing, terrified at the blur of images and collisions as Black tried to slow the car to give him the best chance of carrying out his plan. Then, just as he saw the opening, the windscreen starred to opaqueness, having suffered too many shocks through the now pummelled metal bodywork.

Black knew he had no chance other than to aim for the hole he had fleetingly seen and now completely blind and with no time to even smash a hole in the windscreen in the fast critical situation, he pulled the wheel round sharply to the left.

'Cover your face!' he cried.

Almost at once the car lurched high over to the left and Black momentarily registered the notion that they had taken off. Disorientated by now he couldn't know that they had turned over while travelling through the air and the next thing they knew the roof was crumpling towards them as the car landed on its roof.

When Black began to come round the first thing he noticed besides the fact that he seemed entombed upside-down in a redesigned car was that the front passenger seat was empty and he could have sworn Katherine had been sitting there. Apart from a heavy banging and a smell of burning it was strangely peaceful and he only idly noticed that blood was dripping from his left hand. He wished the banging would stop and began to realise it was getting a bit warm.

Then the window by his side shattered and he was surprised to see the girl standing upside down. She was saying something but it was difficult for him to take in at first. Eventually he realised it was something about the door and how he had to push It open.

It was when he saw the first flames down, or was it up, by his feet and began to cough on the noxious black fumes that he finally began to wake up. He tried to open the door but although he freed the catch he couldn't get any purchase on it due to being trussed up in the seat belt.

For a second or two he couldn't make out how to free himself, so disorientated had his position made him. Then he heard the girl shouting again. She was tugging at the door right next to him; only then did he hear what she was saying. 'Please, please, David. You've got to get out. You must. The car's on fire,' she cried in desperation, great gobbing tears rolling down her cheeks.

At last he understood. Still he wrestled with the seat-belt but he attacked the problem more logically now, tracing the constricting braid back across his hunched form to the buckle. His eyes were watering now as the smoke stung painfully and once when he put his good hand on the metal dashboard for leverage he immediately withdrew it so hot had it become. Now he couldn't see in the billowing smoke as he coughed and choked and lashed out at the buckle with increasing impatience.

Then it was free and as he collapsed in the foetal position the last of his air was expelled from his lungs and he knew that he had only a minute at the most before he would literally began to die of asphyxiation. Already he felt the sickness well up as his body cried out for air. He tried again with the door. It was no use, it wouldn't even budge.

His sensations were fading now and he began to hear a tone in his ears. It was then that he knew he had only one chance. He had no way of knowing if his route of escape was on fire but he must try it anyway or fry along with the vehicle. Choking uncontrollably, having unconsciously taken a great gulp of the foul air, he lunged crazily for the spot where he believed the passenger door to be. Immediately, he became aware of an increase in temperature, which seemed to burn his face and he was dimly aware of yellow flame no more than inches from his eyes. And he was stuck, unable to move any further.

Fighting back hysteria, he patiently tore away a pocket of his jacket, which had caught on something and burst out of the blackness and into clean cool air. As he fought to get his lungs working again he was only marginally aware of the girl's presence and it wasn't until a few minutes later that he realised she had completed the escape he had started, by pulling his legs clear of the blazing car and then rolling him away to safety.

Chapter Nine

It was twenty minutes before Black felt well enough to move, begrimed by oily smoke, with his cut hand wrapped in a far from clean handkerchief that had doubled as a face cloth. Even then, as they started off into the mist away from the burned-out car, he was still coughing, knowing he wasn't really ready but also realising that spending more time than was necessary on the open moor, which was being pelted with sleet, was a sure invitation for trouble, especially as they had no protective clothing to keep out the cold and damp. It had only taken a glance at the wreckage of the car to know nothing was recoverable. Even the mobile phone, trapped in its housing on the dashboard, was now an unrecognisable lump of charcoal.

The obvious route to take would be to just follow the road but Black knew that it was many miles before they would come to any shelter that way. Instead, and realising the inherent danger attending his plan, he decided they must set off cross-country towards the point where the meandering track looped back towards them before heading straight away to a small hamlet a few miles on. It would be a long hard slog in any case, he knew, and the mist would probably make short work of his navigation, but desperate straits required desperate measures and so with all the encumbrances fully realised they strode slowly into the mist and away from the road.

For a while, they said nothing. The sleet at times turned to hailstones, which stung the face and even the shoulders as it bounced off the flimsy clothes they wore. But the cold, the soaking, and the disorientation of stumbling about in near zero visibility were not just problems of discomfort, they were also the ingredients of exposure, a danger which could only arrive more quickly by their silence. Black remembered that it was essential in such circumstances to keep involved so as to avoid the slide into disinterest which too often accompanied exposure.

There was little he could do toward this end beyond talk but he started a conversation that lasted for the next hour and covered so many diverse subjects that long before the end they were feeling in better spirits and hardly noticing the difficulties of squelching over rough moorland.

At one stage, the girl touched upon the question of what had happened to the car.

For Black's part, he had avoided the question before because he hadn't yet come to a final decision. With the car burned out and still hot to the touch an inspection of the braking system had been out of the question. Yet he had the nagging thought that it had not been an accident. He had reflected that until they had arrived at the dam no hint of trouble had been evident. Perhaps it was desperation but he was beginning to tie in the disappearance of the small boat on the reservoir with the brake failure. In the end however he had to realise that he hadn't enough information to come to a logical conclusion on the incident.

But he didn't tell the girl all this. He saw no reason to further worry her, she had surely been through enough. They both had. So he had responded to her question to the effect that these things happen and it was just cruelly unfortunate that it should occur in such a potentially dangerous location.

For perhaps the fifth time, Katherine brought her mobile phone from her pocket and looked at the display. 'Still no signal,' she said.

'You may as well switch it off and conserve the battery,' was Black's response. 'We're nowhere near a mast out here.'

It was getting on for nine-thirty and Black was beginning to doubt the wisdom of his decision to leave the road when they first came upon some shooting butts, followed about ten minutes later by the appearance of a small shooting-box. It wasn't much, just a large wooden shed with the barest attempt to make it homely but once Black had forced the lock any dampness inside was summer weather compared with the horrible conditions outside.

'It'll do,' decided Black after a quick glance around. 'If we can get a fire going we should be able to dry our clothes. Perhaps by then the weather will have improved and we'll be able to see where we're going.'

The girl was already fiddling with the black stove-pipe fire. 'Have you any idea where we are?'

Black smiled at the look with which she accompanied the remark, their new surroundings improving his humour. 'Who says I was ever lost?'

It was the girl's turn to smile. 'You never actually admitted it but..'

'Well, I was possibly not absolutely positive of our exact location but I happened to look at the map of this area last night and I've just placed that large bunch of trees outside.' At that point he jerked a thumb at the window and the fir trees only yards beyond. 'There was only one section of commercial forest in this area and this is it.'

The girl had found the matches by this time and was applying a flame to a hastily set fire. 'And what about the period between the car and when you first saw the forest?'

'You mean, was I lost? Tut tut, Miss Ross. Have you no faith in me?'

The girl came over and stood close to him, a strange expression on her face. 'Plenty,' she said, and smiled. 'You'd better get those wet clothes off and wash away the grime,' she said.

'Yes, nurse.'

She looked around her and when her gaze alighted on the box-bed at one end of the hut, she turned back to him. 'Then you can keep warm by going to bed.'

Black's singed eyebrows gave him an odd appearance but he still managed to convey incredulity. 'What? In those damp sheets without a hot-water bottle?'

'I'll think of something,' she answered mysteriously and then astounded Black by going straight over to the door and sliding the two heavy bolts home.

'Expecting someone, are we?' he asked mischievously, but like the girl he began to get undressed.

'Doesn't seem to be clearing,' observed Black peering through one of the tiny windows of the hut almost an hour later.

Near the fire the girl felt their wrinkled clothes which were draped over anything which afforded proximity to the stove. 'Well at least these are dry and we can get dressed now.'

'And only a while ago you couldn't wait to get them off,' grinned Black turning from the window.

'Funnee,' she said pulling a face, which then went blank in response to Black's sign for silence.

For a moment she strained to hear what he had heard but whatever it was eluded her. But it also eluded Black now because he soon shrugged his shoulders and began to dress.

'You hear all sorts of noises out in the country,' said the girl, trying to explain away the incident. 'When I first came to stay with Uncle Timmie, I couldn't sleep. All those bird noises and the way the mist echoed the sounds of streams. Normally inaudible...'

Being engrossed in tugging on the dry clothing she hadn't been looking Black's way as she spoke but then she became aware of his moving and, now fully dressed, towards the door. At her glance he made a circular motion with his hand which she interpreted as meaning she should continue speaking. This she did, exploring every nuance of her chosen subject, as she watched Black. With painstaking care he drew back the bolts on the door. Once or twice she saw him wince as a bolt rasped in its housing but soon he had both bolts free. Then she stopped talking as he pushed the door outwards and open.

What she saw made her take a sharp breath. There were two men standing just back from the doorway, each attired in storm clothing and neither looked the type who made social calls. But if she was shocked at their unexpected appearance she was astounded by what they said.

It was the smaller of the two who stepped forward immediately Black had pushed open the door. 'David Black, I hope,' he said as the rainwater dripped down the yellow garment to form a pool on the floor. Then he turned to the girl. 'And Miss Ross.'

Black's eyes narrowed. 'That's a mean party-trick of yours. But what brings you here and how do you know our names?'

'It isn't a party trick,' said the other man, stepping into the hut and closing the door behind him. 'The Chairman put out the word that he has important news for you and wants to see you as soon as possible. We're part of the search party that has been looking for you up here.'

'What is it about?' asked Black wanting to get to the important questions first.

'No idea,' said the little one. 'It's just important enough to have us roaming the moors looking for you.' He smiled a boyish grin then which looked oddly out of place on his thin face. 'I must admit finding your car in such a state had us a little worried for a while.'

'Until you could find no signs of the bodies, you mean,'

The little man nodded watching Black closely. 'Just doing a job of work.' He then crossed to the window and looked out briefly. 'As it is, we shouldn't try leaving just yet or we might end up with our car in the same state.'

'You have a car nearby?' asked the girl, eagerness in her voice. 'There's a road?'

'Not more than two-hundred yards away, but we had a few close shaves on the way up. I'd prefer to wait a while before trying to get down again.'

'How long do you suppose we'll have to stay here?'

'Hard to say, Miss. I've lived around here for some years. Could be an hour or it could be twelve. That's what it's like in the hills.'

Black nodded. 'Then we'll just have to wait and see,' he said. 'Make yourself comfortable.'

As the two men stripped off the foul-weather clothing the suspicion Black had begun to feel on first sighting the two men turned into unmitigated distrust. There had been something familiar about their faces even though the heavy PVC hoods had obscured a part of their portraits. Now he was sure he had seen them before and with this reali-sation came that which began to suspect their stat-ed reason for being there.

Then the girl spoke, Black knowing even before she began what she was going to say. 'Haven't I seen you somewhere before?'

The little man stopped what he was doing then and turned to face the girl. 'Of course,' he an-swered, as if the same thought had just entered his head, 'I think I must have seen you in the bar at the *George*. We often go down for a drink or two when we're not working up here.'

As the little one and the girl talked Black began to believe he had been overly suspicious for the man had just admitted to being in the *George* on occasion, the place Black had seen the two men on the afternoon of his arrival. Was it only yesterday? But he had seen the other man at the Garrison Chemical Company premises driving a fork-lift truck as well. What was the Chairman doing launching a mass search party? And why if it was so important he should see the Chairman were they settling into a long stay at the hut instead of striving to return to civilisation and the promised interview?

Then Black saw something that struck an alarm bell in his head. Thinking he was obscured from their view by the little man's frame the other man was taking off his cagoule. He didn't seem to be making a very good job of it either because he had the bulkiness of a parka beneath it which impeded his efforts. It was as he struggled to get the cagoule over his head that one side of the parka flopped open slightly and Black had glimpsed a most familiar metal object.

For a second he wasn't completely certain and was on the verge of believing that he was seeing things. Then, as the minutes ticked by in the warm hut, he began to realise that the man was not going to remove the heavy parka and knew that only if he were trying to hide something would he endure the sweat and discomfort it must be causing him.

As the general conversation continued Black joined in and began to put the newcomers at their ease. Once or twice he even cracked jokes with them but for some of the time he was trying to judge if the little man also was carrying a weapon, a task in which he failed. And all the time he was thinking.

He was beginning to find answers, too. They all depended on a fair amount of speculation but from them emerged something of a pattern. Supposing the two men in the boat had been watching Black's every move and followed him up into the hills. He knew it was stretching possibility but couldn't they work out his destination after some miles and get there more quickly by another route? That begged the question of where they had got the fishing tackle and the boat. A dead end there, reflected Black; it was stretching probability so far that it had snapped.

Then he wondered if the two men had just followed him and, while he and the girl had been in the valve-house, tampered with the brakes on his car. Possible? Could be, for he speculated that the brakes had indeed been tampered with.

Perhaps the two men had then followed them down expecting to see them both dead. Realizing there were no charred remains recognizable as once having been human they might have begun a search, ending in their arrival a few minutes ago. At this point Black realised that if all this were true they must know quite a lot of what was going on. It may be that they had picked on the Chairman as an alibi for being there simply by observing him and Black together. If that were the only reason, why where they here and, more importantly, why had they wanted to kill them or at least put them out of circulation with injuries for a while?

Speculation though all this might be, Black's most pressing problem was to know just what the two men's intentions were if they weren't as stated. Were they just wanting to keep them out of circulation for a while or did they want to get rid of them? The fact that the big man had a gun could sway either argument and for a while Black struggled with speculation as to the reality of the situation. In the end he had no other alternative but to consider the latter. If in doubt consider the worst, was his reasoning. He had to believe that their intention was to kill himself and the girl. It was therefore obvious that he must try to stop it by any means.

This decision brought in another of his rules; that if unarmed and faced with a man with a gun the only sensible course of action is to run. Such an idea was simple. But not if he had to take the girl with him. Here he was with two men against him, one with a gun, and not only was he unarmed he had the burden of looking after a girl as well. It was towards a solution to this problem that he concentrated his attention over several minutes.

'Are you all right, David?' asked the girl, her tone cheerful at the prospect of getting back to Wicklees in a few hours. 'You've suddenly gone all quiet.'

Black was well aware of the intense interest shown to this remark by the two men and knew that a good answer was important. He decided not only to give an excuse but one which would give him an edge later. 'Keep thinking of the car,' he responded, his tone depressed. 'I'm a scientist, not an action-man and I can tell you the experience fair shook me up.'

Black accepted the reassurances of the others in the character he was trying to project and even managed to induce a whine into his voice, the better to persuade them of his tameness. Then, when he was convinced he had milked the most from the situation, he moved into action.

First, he excused himself, saying he had to step outside for a moment. Everyone understood and the big man even said that he too needed to 'get some fresh air'. Black had allowed for this and would have been very surprised as well as disappointed had the big man failed to accompany him in his stated search for relief.

Outside Black led the way around the side of the hut. Then he turned to face the wall, the big man round the corner being just out of view but no more than six feet away. Black waited, listening for the tell-tale signs that the other man was involved in what he was doing. It was then that he struck.

In two strides he was around the corner and lashing out at the man's face. The big man stood no chance. Black's ploy had the most ancient trick in the book as its basis for there is no doubt that it is when a man is relieving himself that he is at his most vulnerable. The thought of any other action at the same time is against instinct and therefore takes time to assimilate. Black took advantage of this law and while the big man was still floundering in the unfairness of his action Black was beating him to the ground.

Black never realised what gave the alarm. Perhaps the man had involuntarily kicked against the hut wall as he had gone down. But there was no doubt that the little man came around the hut just as Black was parting the gun from the now supine figure, jerking up to onto one knee in his haste. Simultaneously he glimpsed the fleeting image of shiny steel and felt a puff of wind as a knife shot mere millimetres in front of his eyes.

As he brought the gun to bear the little man disappeared around the hut again, and Black felt a lull in the sensation of excitement as he realised what the man's intention must surely be. The thought gave his feet wings for he was going round the same corner within a pair of seconds, and was at the open doorway as the little man was dragging the girl to his feet.

Black crossed the room with similar speed and was jabbing the barrel of the gun into the little man's neck even before the girl's shielding body was in place.

Black said just two words as the man's face showed his agony and fright. 'Release her!'

The little man did exactly as instructed but with a little more force than was necessary. The sudden movement upset the girl's balance in the process, so much so that as Black backed away with the gun-barrel trained on the man she fell against his arm knocking him off aim.

With a gleam in his eyes, the little man saw his opportunity and lashed out at Black's wrist with the edge of his hand. There was nothing Black could do. With the girl between him and the man he couldn't properly see his adversary's actions and knew only that the gun had gone spinning from his hand to he knew not where. There was only one thing for it now: escape!

Brutally he whipped the girl around to propel her through the open doorway. Then aware that the little man was already-scrabbling for the gun on the floor he followed her and shouted to her to head for the forest, barely visible in the mist. But he didn't follow. Instead he stepped to one side where the door lay almost flat against the outer wall. Then he listened until he heard the little man's footsteps. From his vantage Black could see about two feet inside the hut and it was when he saw the shape of the figure loom up to this position that he slammed the door to with all his might.

What the immediate result of this was he didn't pause to find out but instead tore after the girl. But he did know that the door hit something softer than the wooden surround. Seconds later they were entering the uneven ground of the forest.

It was difficult making headway against the pattern of deep ditches and low branches of terrain made more hazardous by the scattering of large boulders. Black also realised that not only would they wear themselves out they could easily-become lost because there was no overall slant to the ground which would help them keep going in one direction. He could see them going around in circles and bumping into the two men who he was sure would not be far behind them.

Then he saw a clump of boulders, some as big as a bus, and he decided if they could find a hiding place in there they had a chance of being undetected. It was a chance only and it seemed they no longer had a choice for already he could hear the sounds of movement around them and the occasional voice. Silently, they made for the centre of the grey mass and, in no time, were ensconced beneath a large slab-like overhang, in a space that had only one entrance.

No sooner had Black settled in than the coughing caused by the fire and irritated by the misty air began to return. Also, when he was not concentrating on this, he realised that with only one entrance to their hiding place there was only one exit. It only needed one of the men to hear him cough once, or sight them from the entrance, and the place would be as good a grave as any.

As they listened, Black fighting down the urge to cough and almost choking in the process, they heard the voices getting closer. Shortly they seemed to be coming from directly above them, a suspicion confirmed when a small stone clattered down the wall and struck the girl on her head.

She might have called out at the shock but she was given no such chance. Black's injured left hand clamped solidly over her mouth then, cutting off the expected sound.

They could hear the voices clearly now and listened to the two men as they planned their search. This went on for some time, the two listeners swinging their heads as they tracked the positions of the hunters. Then Black's ears pricked up further as he heard one of them, he presumed the smaller of the two, say quite clearly, 'Big A isn't going to like this one little bit.'

'Unless we find them,' put in the other.

Then although Black listened carefully he heard nothing else for some seconds. Quietly he moved to the entrance and looked out. He knew it was a very dangerous move but, if the next stage of his plan was to work, he needed to take the risk.

A moment's glance brought its reward for not only did he see the two men without being observed himself, he saw they were fading into the mist over to his right and along the easiest path through the trees.

Quickly he grabbed the girl's arm and pulled her out. Then he continued over to the left and in the opposite direction to that taken by the two men. Behind him the girl stumbled several times at the speed she had to go, still tethered to him by his grip. It was only when they were completely engulfed in the closely bunched trees that he let go and slowed the pace.

But he still didn't allow talk, even to explain what was happening and the girl found that she was still no wiser in this respect than she had been just before the fight, discounting the fact she was in some considerable danger.

Within two minutes they came to the edge of the forest again where they saw a fire track. Then Black felt pressure on his arm and looked round to follow the girl's gaze. Just visible was a car, Black's objective, and without delay they crept along the edge of the forest until they were as close as they could get without leaving their cover.

Black knew that it was a possibility that the driver had left the keys in the ignition if for no other reason than that it was unlikely anyone was around to see it, never mind steal it. But given that this possibility existed Black also knew he would only find out by running over to the car and in order to make certain, There was the rub. For if the keys were not in the ignition and the two men appeared on the scene they would have no chance of escape again.

In the fleeting maelstrom of thoughts, which passed through his mind in a bid for an alternative strategy, Black knew they had to take the chance or drift around in the mist for many hours, and probably stumble on the two men in the process. Once he had decided this, he didn't hesitate more than the five seconds necessary to indicate his intentions to the girl before setting his sights on their destination.

They ran, and throughout the time it took for him to cross the twenty yards to the car, to jerk open the door and search frantically for the ignition keys he knew that the next thing he might feel was the impact of a bullet - assuming he felt it at all. As it was the keys were there and so quickly did he start the car and race from the spot that the girl's door was still flapping in the wind some distance along the road.

Chapter Ten

Their descent into better visibility almost half-an-hour later was long overdue for both of them. After their experience with Black's car and the escape, the effect of their surroundings on the nervous system, particular the girl's, was profound.

'Don't waste your time,' said Black, as Katherine tried once again to get a signal on her mobile phone.

With this, she replaced it in her pocket. 'No matter, the battery is almost dead,' she said.

'Try the glove compartment,' he instructed. 'There may be a map.'

'*Voilà*,' she announced, unfolding an ordnance survey map. Without hesitation she began trying to interpret the location of the rain-lashed landmarks around them.

It was only a minute-or-so later that they came across a signpost. It indicated the directions for several unheard-of places. Then, only a few minutes passed along the bumpy road before the girl stabbed at the map with a finger and proclaimed she knew where they were.

Following Black's distracted congratulations - the distraction caused by the need for him to concentrate on driving through the slushy, pot-holed lane - she turned her attention to things a little further from survival.

'The next thing we must do is find a police station,' she announced eagerly, her head once more in close proximity to the map. 'A phone would do, wouldn't it? And there is one marked as being no more than, let me see... Four miles away, if you turn right at the next cross-roads.'

'Forget it,' said Black, still peering through the drenched windscreen whose wipers managed only to give *hope* of seeing clearly and not certainty. 'I have pressing business in Wicklees.'

The girl's tone was incredulous. 'But they'll get away. If we just stop and call the police they could be up there in no time.'

Black sighed, the tiredness from lack of sleep and action serving to shorten both his patience and his temper. With some surprise he realised he hadn't slept properly since the night before the incident which though incredibly only the previous day seemed ages ago, and he supposed lack of food might have something to do with it. 'Look, I said forget it. A detour will take time and petrol and as you still haven't told me anything apart from where we were a few minutes ago, I still don't know if I'm travelling in the right direction or how far we have to go to get to Wicklees!'

In the silence that followed - as the girl angrily searched the map for the information he had indicated - Black looked over at her mess of hair and mud-streaked clothes and knew he didn't have the right to take it out on her when not only had she shared so much with him these past few hours but had also contributed to saving his life in the burning car. Silently he placed a hand on her leg and squeezed. When she turned to him, tears looming in her eyes, he managed a smile.

Then he turned back to watch the road again. 'Besides,' he continued, 'I have no intention of telling the police anything until I'm ready.'

Once again the girl's reaction was incredulity. 'Don't tell me you don't even trust the police.'

'All right, I won't,' he responded without looking round.

'This is no time for flippancy, David. Two people tried to kill us up there. We have to tell the police.'

'Normally I would agree. I have the utmost faith in the police but...'

'But what?'

'But I happen to have my reservations about two of them as far as keeping their mouths shut and, by extension, whether their involvement is deeper.' As he said this he thought of the words he had heard through the door of the bar at the *George* and his discovery that they had been spoken by one of the policemen.

The girl tried to discover who he was talking about but he wouldn't say. Again there was silence, at least as far as conversation went because the rain on the metal of the car and the splash of water and grit on the under-body did not conjure the feeling of peace. A few seconds later she produced her conclusions from the map by saying they had six miles to go to Wicklees along the road they were on, before lapsing once more into silence as she stared ahead.

It didn't last long and what she said served to prove that she was still brooding on his intransigence.

'You don't trust anyone, do you,' she said calmly, presenting a statement not a question.

'I've already told you, Katherine. Until I'm certain, everyone is under suspicion.'

'How can you be like that?'

Black shrugged. 'It's my job. I could have been killed many times without this rule. We might have...' He paused then for a second before continuing, 'Well, you saw what happened up in the hills.'

Again they fell into silence and Black got around to thinking just what he would be doing in Wicklees apart from having a very interesting interview with Lord Alland. He had to get rid of the girl, of course. He must find her a place of safety, and one where he knew she would be under constant surveillance. Then he could get back to working alone as he preferred to and not for the first time he wondered at the constrictions his decision to look after the girl had caused. In any case, if his feelings were not upset by ever stronger notions concerning her, he meant to continue their liaison.

'When we get to Wicklees we're going straight to the *George*,' he said, after a time. 'Then we'll go up to your room where you'll pack your things and keep your door locked until I return. Then I'll pick you up an hour later and take you to a place of safety well away from all this.'

'You don't trust me either, do you?' was her response.

'I've already told you that I do!' he barked, his expression very serious. 'Now don't argue. I've already managed to place your life in danger on three occasions and I'm not prepared to do it again. You will stay with my aunt until I say it is safe for you to leave.'

What she thought of this wasn't something she was prepared to say for she remained silent all through the time it took to get to the inn and for Black to escort her to her room.

'Don't forget, 'he said, turning for the door after she had ignored his attempted embrace, 'Keep the door locked and don't open it to anyone but me. I'll be back in an hour.'

Black didn't immediately return to the car but went along to his own room where he hastily changed into the remnants of his wardrobe and retrieved another mobile phone from one of the locked cases.

Out in the car park he looked back once towards the window of the girl's room although he saw no sign of her. But as he sped down the lane the girl appeared at the window to watch him go, a pensive expression on her face.

Katherine Ross's expression would most certainly have been different had she known what Black was thinking as he sped towards Highfields Hall. If he had entertained any doubt over Lord Alland's complicity in the further developments surrounding the poisoning incident they were being quickly discarded. And the girl was the principal reason.

He had never managed to reconcile the prompt appearance of the two men on the moor with anything other than the result of inside information. The Chairman hadn't known he was on his way to the dam. In fact John Arrowsmith was of the opinion that Black's first task of this day was the errand he was at present engaged upon: visiting Lord Alland. So how did the two men come to know of his visit? And what was their intention? To kill both of them or just Black? He hadn't found an answer to this either, but he could hazard a very good guess. What he was certain of at this stage was that only one other person knew where he was going when he left the inn in the early hours: Katherine Ross.

He didn't wonder now that she was so unafraid when left alone at the inn. He suspected that on both occasions of her being out of his company she had been talking to them. Now it seemed that 'them' included Lord Alland, or as the two men knew him, rather melodramatically, 'Big A.'

Black had no intention of giving any warning of his arrival at Highfields Hall and so he jumped from the car as soon as it had stopped and ran for the door. Even so, Hasker was there before him, which brought another thought to Black's mind concerning the girl's complicity.

Black had no time for the niceties either. 'Where is Lord Alland?' he asked as he brushed past Hasker.

'Out, I'm afraid,' came the reply.

'That's a surprise. Allow me to disbelieve you. Mind if I look for myself?'

'Help yourself. If you must.' Hasker was calmness itself, which Black interpreted as either confirmation of Lord Alland's absence or resignation that things were getting beyond control with this man who lacked manners. But it struck Black as odd that the man hadn't threatened to call the police, a most natural response surely when someone was forcing their way into such a showroom of priceless antiques.

With Hasker in tow Black visited every room of the house, ending finally at the study. He found no sign of Lord Alland along the way but in this last room discovered a map with all the factories marked in pen. Most were circled in blue but one, very heavily marked in red, was the factory he had visited himself: The Garrison Chemical Company.

Using Lord Alland's telephone he made several calls until he managed to contact the audit team. He could have saved his time by just calling Garrison as it was there that the audit team was still working. Briefly Black told the head man to keep them there until he arrived. Then he rooted around for a few more seconds in the same drawer he had found the map before deciding this was the only thing he wanted and ran from the house.

Out on the road he looked at his watch. He had promised the girl he would be back in an hour and already he had used up twenty-five minutes of that. Now he had to go up into the hills again to the factory. He was going to be late, he thought, with a shrug, and turned onto the road that would lead him to Garrison. He couldn't realise just what the consequences of being late would be.

At the factory twenty minutes later he met Johnson, the man in charge of the audit team.

'What news?' asked Black.

It had been a long hard slog doing both the first lightning audit and following it hours later with another, longer version. It showed very completely in the way the man said, quite simply. 'Nothing.'

'Nothing whatsoever?'

'Nothing more than was indicated in our first report,' he answered, a steeliness coming to his voice. 'No more than a litre or two at each factory and certainly nowhere near a drum-load. I'd like to get my hands on the man who had us waste our time going through all this lot again, I'll tell you.'

Black didn't bother to illuminate Johnson on this point. 'Look at this map,' he said, dragging out the badly folded sheet from under his arm. 'You can see that this place is circled in red while all the rest are circled in blue. Doesn't that seem significant if an anti-polluter was the one who did it?'

Johnson nodded but it was obvious from his expression that he couldn't say how, having found nothing there, and he said so.

'How much were you told to look for?'

Johnson shrugged his shoulder, the black circles under his eyes not giving much emphasis to the gesture. 'A drum-load we were told. But what are you getting at?'

'In a moment.' reassured Black. 'First tell me if you've taken a full inventory of all the chemicals, raw materials if you like, that have been used in this factory over the last year.'

'We've been through the books, of course. But what has this to do with missing chemicals?'

'Just this. Suppose we've got the scale wrong. Instead of a drum-load being missing let's say it is a whole batch.'

At this Johnson's eyes began to light-up. 'I see. You want to find out what substances have been used to produce chemicals in the past year,'

'Right.. And it may not only be TCP that we're looking for. It may be that a higher yield of TCDD was produced than is legal and all of it was collected together. Then it might be that we're not just looking at a drum-load of TCP we're looking at many drum-loads of TCDD.'

Johnson's face fell. 'You frighten me, Black. I hope to God you're miles off the track, but I'll start my men on it right away. I should have some answers for you very quickly. Are you staying?'

'Haven't time,' replied Black, folding the map again. 'Pass whatever news you have through the Chairman.' At that he turned away and walked quickly to his car.

It had just gone noon when he got back to the inn. There was a bustle about the place with several of the pop concert people mingling in the foyer as Black mounted the stairs. On the way he noticed the landlord puffing along, red-faced, onto the same landing as that which served the girl's room but selecting another room as his destination at the opposite end of the corridor where he stopped and knocked on a door. By the time Black began to tap lightly on the girl's door the publican had disappeared into the other room.

Black knew within seconds that something was wrong because he got no response whatsoever to his entreaties for her to open the door. Presently the cleaning woman who he had heard explain the break-in to the police appeared around the door of the adjacent room.

'What's all the row about?' she asked.

'Have you seen Miss Ross?'

'I should say I have. They want me to go on in the restaurant because of her. Running out like that. It's not fair.'

Black asked her to explain what she was talking about.

'Gone she has,' she explained, in the tone one would use with a particularly slow child. 'Ten minutes ago. Her and the squire. I've got to do her shift and my Henry doesn't know anything about it...'

Black interrupted. 'You say Lord Alland was here? She left with him?'

''Course I did. You deaf?' She didn't really expect confirmation or denial on this point for at that point she lost her patience with him and shut the door in his face.

As Black wandered back down the corridor on his way to his room he tried to think of the implications of this latest blow. He didn't get far in this for as he approached the stairs which led to his room he saw again Appleton's stout frame. The landlord was on his way back down the corridor and he looked as if he had seen a ghost. So much was he taken up with his own thoughts that he didn't even notice Black, but just walked past him seemingly in a trance.

Black wasn't in quite such pronounced shock and it struck him in a blinding flash that the girl might not have left with Alland at all but for some unexplainable reason be in the room just vacated by the landlord. At the thought Black changed course for the other room and so impatient was he to know if he was right he just turned the doorknob and walked in.

Within five seconds he was on his way out. A glance had established that the girl wasn't present. Then all he wanted to do was get away from the old woman and the severe-looking waitress who were there and who also were understandably shocked by his unannounced entrance. He still saw the scene as he walked quickly down the corridor; of the bed-ridden old woman with those old-fashioned eye-covers, which supposedly helped her sleep, and the look of fear on the face of the woman.

His mind was still in some turmoil when he arrived at his room and opened the door. For a moment he just stood there, leaning against the doorjamb. In front of him and on the dressing table were the remains of what once had been his computer. Everything else apart from the stool was as it had been when he had last spent time there, but the stool had been dismantled in the course of battering the machine. It was some few seconds before he decided there was nothing worth staying there for and turned again for the stairs.

He had been feeling a little better on his way back from Garrison. He knew he wasn't on top of the situation at that time but he felt that now he was alone he could begin to make an impression. It had taken just five minutes to destroy the quiet confidence that he had sorely needed. During the time it took him to descend to the unusually crowded foyer he toyed with the idea of trying to carry on alone but he knew it was no use. He needed help. He would have to talk to the Chairman.

For several minutes he waited impatiently while what seemed a conference of people finished with the only working telephone in the foyer. Deep though Black's thoughts were at the time he couldn't help but be aware of the commotion around him. It seemed the pop concert organisers had a problem and their spokesman was relaying to and from the telephone just what was being discussed. Something about their concert site being water-logged or something, Black realised, and the heated communications were an attempt to establish another. On and on went the negotiations and louder and louder grew the attendant din and histrionics.

After Black began to realise that at least a third of the crowd were also waiting their turn for the telephone he gave up and strolled out into the street in search of a phone box. He was sorely tempted to ignore his rule and use the mobile phone but discipline prevailed.

It had stopped raining now but the sky was still full of dark rain clouds, which threatened to open up at any time, the whole effect creating a depressive atmosphere of the type that could tempt suicide in those most at risk.

Black gave it no more than a glance and knowing the nearest public telephone was in Wicklees itself, he headed for the car park. He was not the suicidal type, fortunately. He knew that things had suddenly gone completely against him and that he was now back at square one. He was back at the bottom of a long ladder and there was only one direction he could go, up.

But he was wrong. The car was gone.

It said a lot for his character that he merely shrugged at the possibility that the two men who

had tried to kill him were now in the vicinity and
without hesitation he turned for the road and the
short walk to Wicklees.

Chapter Eleven

'Kind of you to take the trouble to tell me!' said the voice at the other end of the line, which Black recognized unmistakably as that of the Chairman. He didn't miss the heavy sarcasm either, which was in response to the brief *résumé* of Black's recent movements Black had just related. And even though he had edited his story quite ruthlessly so that the barest sketch reached his boss, he knew it still made pretty bad listening.

'You lost contact for over twelve hours,' accused Arrowsmith heatedly, and Black had to admit the truth in that.

'You lost the girl, who you say is somehow involved with the present situation.' Accurate enough there, thought Black in silence.

'You have failed to contribute the slightest hint which would progress this investigation.' Which was also true, admitted Black. It didn't mean he hadn't got ideas, just that he hadn't 'contributed' them to the Chairman's hearing.

'You have also lost the use of an expensive computer by allowing 'persons unknown' to alter its volumetric parameters.' Black could see him ticking off the points on his fingers and realised that the way he was going he would soon have to change hands.

And Arrowsmith was still 'going'. 'Above all you lose Alland, our principal suspect!' Black fielded this one in silence too, although his face registered a chagrined expression when he thought that it had been the Chairman who had diverted his attention from Alland in the first place. And now he was calling him 'our' suspect!

Black allowed him to ramble on, paying little attention now as the man berated him for everything short of the third world war and the only excuse he could find for not pinning that on him too being that it hadn't happened yet. But by his tone such a minor detail as that wasn't going to stop him for long.

Black smiled at this thought and then his mind struck a comparison. Although much of mankind saw the third world war as synonymous with a nuclear devastation that would be all over in the time it takes to smoke a cigarette, the reality was that the *true* Third World War had for a long time been wreaking an increasing destruction on our habitat with the perils of pollution a virtually unchallenged enemy. But it was a different type of war, that he had to concede in the war of pollution there were no human or animal victors. All were losers.

He had no time then to review the thoughts which quickly soured his smile. His comparison had been enabled through the product of years of research: a comparison that at once surprised him and yet stuck him as obvious. He knew that not only was the growth of pollution being virtually unopposed. It was being positively helped along.

And there were many indications of this. One of them was the relaxation of safety rules, that, due to the tortuous economics of a world in recession, forced corner-cutting in safety if a job was to be kept. It seemed to him a missed opportunity that in a state of collapsed world trade the world's factories where run down to minimal production. It had not been realised that here was the time to strengthen the anti-pollution and safety laws to ensure that the industries which later grew large produced at the same time a cleaner, safer environment.

This was a rather oblique example of helping along pollution through failing to think ahead, but there were others that were quite straightforward. Some could have catastrophic consequences even in the short-term. That great medium for measuring the health of the environment, the water supply, was about to be abandoned, as such, as many of this country's water authorities dispensed with the services of scientists employed on water analysis. Now, virtually no region had the services of a full time toxicologist. Dangerous though the TCP was, at least one water authority didn't even test for it in the water supply?

In turn, this thought provoked others and, perhaps influenced by his lack of success in the operation for which the voice in his ear still scolded him, he began to think of the job he had been on before and the rewards it had promised to bring.

He thought of the growing conviction he had felt during the previous ten days that he was within touching distance of a network of polluters who, as members of a 'ring', rigged invoices and cargo notes to move dangerous chemicals around in order to lower overheads and thus boost profits. In Black's scenario-ed third world war he counted these among the 'enemy'.

It had been with deep disappointment that he had responded to his abrupt diversion to this case. Now he wasn't just disappointed, he was mortified that all his work could go for nothing in the breathing space his absence from the hunt had given his opponents.

Then he stopped thinking about it because he had heard something from the telephone that struck an alarm bell in his head. 'What was that?'

'Do me the courtesy of listening, Black,' admonished the Chairman, 'I was saying that Number Ten have been on the line. It appears they have received a message, an ultimatum, from people indisposed to identify themselves. They say unless the Bill goes to a second reading with a large government backing they will poison thousands of people.'

For a moment there was silence on the line. Black was thinking hard, trying to remember what it was about the mention of a Bill that was so important. Then he had It. 'Of course!' he exclaimed, thinking aloud. 'The private members amendments to the Pollution Bill. It gets its first reading today.   I'd forgotten all about it. I suppose, like everybody else, I didn't give it a chance after the government announced its objections.'

'So it seems did these people,' said the Chairman. 'The reading takes place this afternoon but is expected to be followed by a lengthy debate. That is why they gave a deadline of midnight tonight.'

'Midnight! They can't be serious!'

'We can only believe what we are told,' continued Arrowsmith, 'and if we do believe this is a serious plot we have something like ten hours to stop it.'

'But surely the House could pretend to go through the motions of sending the amendments through and stop a second reading at a later date on the grounds of coercion.' But although Black spoke these words he knew even before the Chairman replied that such a manoeuvre would not take place.

'This government is hard-line,' said Arrowsmith. 'Can you see it telling the world that it succumbed to threats. And remember, Black, we still don't know if this plot is for real and not just so much 'hot air'. That is what I told them.'

Black was angry. 'You told them you thought it was a hoax?'

'Not exactly, but I'm still not personally convinced of its authenticity.'

'Have you forgotten the children?' retorted Black, his voice rising. 'I realise they are recovering fast, but we've suffered a fatality. That was no hoax!'

But Arrowsmith didn't continue the point. Instead he muttered distractedly for Black to hold the line.

Black heard a scuffling sound in the ear-piece followed by a hardly audible murmur of voices as the Chairman spoke to others off the line. Stupidity. Damned stupidity to risk lives at all whether the pretext was flimsy and unsubstantiated or not, thought Black, as he waited for the Chairman to return to the telephone. It was too easy to say 'call their bluff' but in a situation like this one they surely needed to take no chances whatsoever. The plan was so possible, it just might be true.

'Black?'

'Yes. I'm still here,' he responded in a voice that started angry but wavered a little as he recognized something in the Chairman's voice. He recognized fear.

'I've just been told you re-directed the aims of the auditing team,' he said slowly, almost distractedly. 'Johnson has just sent a message which is a little ambiguous. He says that a whole batch load of TCP was manufactured but cannot be traced. Furthermore, when he presented this to the management, one confessed that they had been using an old process. Look, Black, what does this mean?'

'I think you have a very good idea, sir. But it means that much more than one drum of chemical is missing. The true figure may be ten, twenty, perhaps a hundred. I don't know, maybe even as many as a hundred drums are missing. And not only that, if it is the old TCP it is extremely dangerous whatever the amount.'

The Chairman's voice was strained. 'This is terrible!'

'That's putting it mildly,' responded Black. 'I think you had better get on the line to Downing Street again, and pretty quickly too.'

'But what do I tell them?'

'Just tell them you were wrong in your last response and ask them to get a toxicologist to explain the effect of several hundred gallons of TCDD diluted to the taste of several thousand people.'

'Of course,' agreed the Chairman, his voice shaking. 'And you? What will you do?'

'You say we've got ten hours. I aim to spend all of them trying to locate and prevent this operation because I have the feeling you may not convince the government in time. But in order to accomplish that I need a car, mine was burned out, remember?' he added, and he noted that the Chairman didn't try to ram this down his throat.

'It'll be with you within the hour. Where do you want it?'

Black told him. He had sounded confident in saying he would try to sort out the dangerous situation but it didn't mirror his feelings for he didn't really know where to start. Finding all the things or people he had lost, as the Chairman had so rightly listed, was probably a task too great for him to accomplish in the few hours available.

He began to think about any straw he could latch onto to keep in touch with the situation. As he walked quickly towards the inn he was engrossed in finding a solution to this problem and by the time he got there he had begun to see a straw at least, but whether he could reach it was another matter.

When he got back to his room he made immediately for the USB storage key he had slid under his bed

What a mess, he thought, and he wasn't just referring to the wrecked computer either. They now had fifty-square miles of reservoir 'country' to search in nine-odd hours. Then he retrieved the USB key and knew he had the 'where' and 'who' information. At least he now had a straw to clutch at, he reflected.

The hope was that the answer was on that USB key, a copy of his research from the laptop, or why would anyone wreck the computer? It showed their ignorance in that they weren't aware there was a copy of his work other than the hard-disk the computer - if indeed they perceived of the fact that it could copy to a USB key at all - but the wrecked computer still indicated that there was something in its use that was incriminating to someone and that was Black's 'straw'.

Now he must review his work of the previous night and, belatedly, look through the 'who' part of the problem.

Time was short and he didn't even know if he could recover the information on the USB key yet, written as it was for the program that wrote it, not universally available. He still must try to review the 'who' research in the process as although he had heaped total blame on the missing Lord Alland, there were bits of the puzzle which didn't fit. Perhaps the 'who' data could tell him. But how, with the computer smashed? Towards solving this problem he quickly left the room, carrying the USB key.

At the desk he found a copy of Yellow Pages and in the comparative quiet of a now almost deserted foyer he flicked through the pages until he found what he wanted. Then he made two telephone calls; one of which was for a taxi.

It was six miles to Handley, the nearest town to Wicklees that boasted the facilities Black needed. The road was quite bad but nevertheless the taxi driver accomplished the trip, door to door, in seven minutes - and Black ventured the thought that the girl believed *he* was a fast driver.

Telling the driver to hang on he crossed a small market square to a shop bearing loud indication that it was a computer sales point. As he opened the door the nearby church clock struck the quarters: quarter- to-two.

It was a quarter-past-two when he emerged, and seconds later he was enduring the self-inflicted punishment of a return high-speed journey in the taxi. However this time it wasn't so exhilarating for he was too preoccupied with the thoughts conjured up by his session with the computer-shop's equipment.

At Wicklees he got out at the call-box he had used to speak with the Chairman and paid off the taxi there. Then he entered the call-box and rang the telephone number of the newspaperman who had first broken the news to the Chairman of the anonymous telephone call. As he waited for the call to be answered he reflected on his latest reasoning.

He was now convinced beyond doubt that Lord Alland was involved with the threatened operation. However he didn't yet know why and this worried him for action without reasonable motive meant either Lord Alland was mad or he, Black, had missed something. But he also pondered on his review of the 'who' disks and was surprised at what he had discovered about the local populace. His call now would add only a minimum of information to that already in Black's head but it could be a key that opened the door to heightened awareness of what the overall picture could be.

Then the journalist came on the line and Black told him what he wanted.

'*Exactly* what was said?' repeated the journalist.

'Exactly,' confirmed Black.

The journalist thought for a moment, and then repeated the message he had later given the Chairman over the telephone.

Black pondered this for a moment, unable to see anything in the message other than the obvious.

'You still there?' prompted the journalist.

'I'm still here,' assured Black. 'Tell me, what did the voice sound like?'

At the description the journalist gave, Black's spirits rose a little. They were to soar later, when he had time to digest the relevancy of it, but for now they rose when the man described Lord Alland's unmistakable voice. And although Black's experience of the voice had been restricted to the mumblings of a man when he was heavily sedated, he knew it was Lord Alland all the same.

'Are you positive about that?'

''Course I am. It's my job to observe and listen. What's so important to you and Mr Arrowsmith that you both doubt my word?'

'Never mind,' answered Black, wanting to go.

'Wait a minute,' urged the journalist. 'Is there a story in this for me?'

Black thought for a moment. 'Might be.'

'Where do I find you when I get up there?'

Black thought distractedly of his movements over the next few hours. He knew he could be anywhere. 'You don't,' he said. 'But stick to Mr Arrowsmith. He'll lead you to where the story is.'

Chapter Twelve

When he got back to the inn he found a man waiting for him, leaning against the car he had brought on the Chairman's instructions. The car was parked directly outside the main entrance and though he gave the keys to Black it was obvious he intended staying.

He must have seen the question in Black's eyes at this for he said, 'Arrowsmith decided you needed help as well as the car you asked for. I'm it.'

Black found the idea of having a watchdog loathsome, but he made certain not to reveal this. 'Great!' he said, relief evident in his tone. 'At last they realise I can't win the war on my own. Welcome to the team.'

With that he stooped to peer through the window of the tail-gate. 'Plenty of room in there,' he announced quizzically. Then he turned to the man. 'Look, we've a hell of a lot of work to do and we've got to do it fast. Ok?'

The man nodded but the questions were showing on his face.

Black plunged a hand into his coat pocket. 'Here's the key to my room. Inside is a wrecked jumble of electrics that used to be a computer and I need to take it to Handley to get the hard-disk out of it. Bring the whole caboodle down, will you?'

Again the man nodded, accepting Black's room-key.

Then after Black had lifted open the car's tail-gate, he ushered the man towards the inn, fetching his mobile phone from his pocket. 'I've got an important call to make first but I'll be up to give you a hand as soon as I've finished,' he added, allowing the man to go ahead of him to the door.

With that they passed through the main entrance and into the foyer and as Black turned his back on the room and pretended to make a call, the man continued for the stairs. Black waited only long enough for the man to disappear from view before replacing the mobile phone in his pocket and heading back to the door.

At the car, he slammed the tail-gate shut before hurriedly climbing behind the wheel and driving away.

The road he chose would have taken him back towards Handley but that was not his intended destination. He had kept an eye on his rear-view mirror for the period when the inn was still in view but as soon as he got the opportunity he took a turning which would put him on the right road for Highfields Hall.

Black's main intention in getting rid of the man by his ruse had been an instinctive repulsion to crowds, and he felt even two people was a crowd if he hadn't chosen the company of the other person. Now he was on the road and had time to think, he began to wonder about the man. On reflection he realised the stranger hadn't asked any questions when instructed to go to Black's room. And to Black this seemed odd. The keys of the *George* were not of the type that boasted a cricket-bat sized fob bearing room-number and ancillary information. Instead, it was a miniscule tally on his key, which bore a small none-too-readable imprint of the number eighteen. If Black remembered rightly, the man hadn't even glanced at it.

Such speculation suggested the man not only knew his room number but, when he had unerringly headed for the stairs, also the layout of the inn and therefore the whereabouts of his room.

Then he wondered about the complete absence of reaction to his references to a wrecked computer. With this, Black had to assume the man had visited his room before, and perhaps it had been him who had re-shaped his machine.

But all this was speculation, and he knew he hadn't time for such luxuries with only hours to go. Black determined with an effort to get his mind back on the problems of reality, as near as they were visible to his mind's eye.

He was returning to Lord Alland's house yet again because of such a reality. Black had no doubts that Alland was in this thing up to his neck. Now he was going to tell Black all about it if he had to break that self-same neck in the process.

Although Black believed pure bad luck to be the reason he had missed him on his last visit, when it coincided with Lord Alland picking up the girl, he wasn't taking any chances this time.

Rather than cruise up to the main entrance with the stealth of a fire-engine responding to an emergency, and thereby allowing the Highfields fraternity the opportunity of escape via the back entrance, he decided on a quieter approach.

He was still some way from boundary wall when he stopped the car and parked it where it couldn't be seen from the road. Then he leapt the wall with a little difficulty before moving as quietly as possible through the band of shrubbery that covered most of the few hundred yards between him and the house.

Within five minutes of entering the property he was at the rear wall of the house and with his face up against a window. He recognised the room from his tour but there was something different about it now, for although it was deserted the furnishings seemed less substantial. But he didn't worry about this for the present, his concentration was focused on finding a way in without being detected and therefore maintaining the element of surprise.

He tried the window then but found he couldn't budge it. Then he tried another, and another, but the result was always the same. Finally he came to a door and swiftly took up a position on the hinged side so that he would be unseen if it were opened.

For a moment he stood still, his head pressed close to the door as he listened for sounds from within. Nothing. He then realised he had neither seen or heard any sign of human life since arriving here and he began to get the same heavy feeling he had experienced when he had found the girl gone and the computer wrecked. He was too late. Again.

Fortunately, the front door was unlocked. A brief glance around the first room he entered confirmed his first suspicions. No longer was this the opulent residence of a rich man, garnished with a priceless collection of antiques. The house had been stripped.

It was also bereft of human life and seemed to have been evacuated in a hurry for the wardrobes in the bedrooms still contained clothes and around lay the trappings of domesticity. Only the valuable items had been taken and there had been a pantechnicon-load of those.

For a while Black drifted from room to room in the hope of finding something different, some clue, but the answer was always the same. In the room he had first seen through the window he saw what it was that was different. This was the library: it was the room in which he had encountered Lord Alland on the previous evening but although the desk was still there the rest of the room was a shambles.

Feeling some of the depression exuded by the scarred walls and littered floor, Black sat heavily in the finely-upholstered chair at the desk. High on the wall opposite were the bright squares and rectangles that, until very recently, had been the locations from which the family-portraiture had gazed down. Only the tallies remained, announcing a family tree going back hundreds of years.

Why do this? What kind of mentality could throw away so much? These were the questions that dominated Black's thinking as he sat back and gazed at the mess.

Only hours before, this house had been a home and a monument to tradition and wealth and heritage. So what was it that had provoked Lord Alland into this desecration? What made any man run?

Fear. Perhaps he, Black, had played a bigger part in this than he had believed. He began to assemble bits of information in his head, trying to build a picture of what had caused Alland to flee. Black had not only been on the road to tracking down a network of polluters in his previous assignment, he had ultimately been seeking to identify the guiding force behind the illegal search for profit. One man, Mr Big, as they said in the movies. But perhaps 'Big A?'

It seemed to fit. Black began to see things more clearly and believed he had at last found the 'motive' which could plausibly identify Alland as the man behind this mad scheme. He now wondered if Alland was mad, or just scared when Black had begun to put the pressure on.

Was that immodest, he wondered? Or was it naive? Black had spent so much time running in circles that he hadn't really had the opportunity to put pressure on anyone! That was what Black now believed, feeling his involvement had been minimal: worrisome interference for a small-time protest group but not enough to do any damage to the big-time polluters.

He was still reflecting upon this when the telephone on the desk rang. For a moment Black debated whether he should answer it but then picked up the receiver and said, simply, 'Hello?'

The man on the other end introduced himself as an organiser of the pop-concert being held locally, a statement borne out by Black's recognition of the voice which had done the relaying of information for the crowd in the foyer of the *George* earlier.

'We'd like to thank you for saving the gig,' said the voice cheerily. 'I mean, without the new site we'd have been washed out. So we thought we'd like to call and say thanks and invite you out here for a look at what's on.'

Black thought furiously. 'Wait a minute, I didn't deal with this one. Where did you say the new site is?'

The man at the other end was confused and the tone of his voice demonstrated this even if it didn't prevent him from answering the question. Black made a note of the location and carried the telephone over to the wall where he peered at a map of the area.

'And you moved from where?'

If the man had been confused by the previous question he was dumbfounded by this last one.

But again, even now that a wariness had crept into his voice, he answered.

Black thanked him tersely and declined the offer of a tour. Then he replaced the receiver and marked the two locations on the map.

For the next ten minutes he pored over the map, having transferred it to the desk. With a new suspicion had come a new dynamism and it made his pulse quicken with anticipation. Throughout this time he formulated his plan and his policy, the latter being that the police could handle finding Lord Alland and the girl while he would concentrate on the target. That the two might be identical did not cross his mind. He saw Lord Alland as a frightened man who was running away after deploying the chemical. In a way he was right, but in a way he was also very wrong.

Then he picked up the telephone and rang Inspector Davies.

'I hope this is important,' answered Davies, 'because I'm absolutely swamped at the moment.'

'The pop concert?'

'The same,' sighed the policeman.

'Well, it just happens that this is about the pop concert, too,' said Black. 'But have you got two or three minutes to hear the full story first?'

'Go ahead.' Davies's voice was impatient.

Four minutes later his tone had changed. 'It's fantastic. Are you kidding me? Lord Alland?'

It was Black's turn to be impatient. 'I haven't the time to go worrying busy police officers with tales of fantasy,' he said, frustration blurring his meaning. 'I've just spent some time with a map and I've got it down to three dams. Only three reservoirs supply the tributaries serving the stream at the pop-concert site.'

'How do you know it is the pop-concert?'

'The ultimatum spoke of killing thousands of people. How many people do you estimate are at this moment dossed down on the banks of that stream?'

'Ten, twelve thousand.'

'And a lot more yet to arrive, no doubt.'

'True.' Davies's tone was changing to seriousness now, the import of what Black was saying gradually sinking in. 'Ok, you want these dams investigated. You realise I've got most of my men involved with policing the crowd at the concert, don't you? I can't spare many.'

Black liked Davies but it wasn't the time for worrying about feelings. 'Look, it's your problem whatever happens.' he said brusquely. 'If you don't send enough men to cover these dams then you can use the ones left behind to bury the bodies!'

If Davies's temper rose at the barb it didn't show in his response. 'All right, I'll sort something out immediately,' he said, tiredly. 'Have you any other ideas.'

'Yes, move the crowd off the site.'

Davies laughed but it wasn't a nice laugh. 'You're joking! We're the enemy in their eyes already, and what with their just having moved from another site which was washed out, they... Oh, all right. As you say, we either move them or bury them.'

Perhaps Black felt some of the weight Davies was under for he then tried to lessen the load. 'Look, I was up at one of the dams this morning. I found nothing of interest there. Perhaps you could skip that one and concentrate what forces you have on the other two.'

'Well, that's something anyway.' responded Davies, with just a little more life in his voice. 'Where are these two dams?'

Black told him. Then, added, 'Just one more thing...'

'*More?*'

'The publican at the inn.'

'Appleton?'

'Yes. There's something pressing on his mind so much that it shows. It was at the inn that the incident took place. There might be a connection. Do you think you could check it out as a matter of urgency?'

Davies sighed. 'I'll stop-by myself on the way to the dams area.'

'Thanks.'

Black felt he could almost find his way back to the dam area blindfolded but he still took the map along for when he needed to branch off to his new destination. There was little vehicular traffic on the road but about four miles outside town he came across a virtually blocked section of road caused by a stream of walkers several hundred strong, a mass of colour in their light-weight storm clothing. Here and there were dotted the day-glow-yellow-and-blue-uniformed police and, more animated, the organisers who cajoled the crowd into order.

A march, that was what it seemed to be, to Black, and as he drove barely above walking pace in the confined space he saw all ages and all colours of skin among the column. Mainly they seemed happy, too, despite the weather, and he could hear through the wound-down window much laughter and giggling. Something about it all affected Black and he began to see that behind all the organisational problems of management and policing was something very worthwhile. Of course, he knew that as with any large crowd a contingent will cause problems; pickpockets, drug-pedlars, vandals. But at least it brought people together.

He had gone a mile from sighting the first stragglers before passing the gap in the high hedge where they turned into a field already swarming with people. Again, their cars and buses well clear of the field, police stood around in groups. He didn't envy their task. A person with even the most gentle of dispositions isn't going to be too keen to move after hours of indecision and upheaval. Multiply that by several thousand and drop in the mystical ingredient called mob mentality and a very ugly confrontation could ensue.

But then he thought of the task facing them if the people where contaminated with the chemical and in response he involuntarily put his foot down hard on the accelerator and began to move quickly along the now empty road.

Now that he could pick up speed he began to think of the route ahead. He was almost at the point where he should turn off onto another road for one of the two dams he and Davies would oversee. He suspected the police were already on their way because although there had been perhaps a hundred police at the concert field, they still seemed very thin on the ground,

For some moments Black tried in vain to read the map and drive at the same time. But it was no use. With the zigzagging of the road it was far too dangerous and so he stopped the car.

Reluctantly, he removed the mobile phone from its pouch and switched it on. Then he set up the GPS app and within seconds he saw that he was getting a signal and then the moving map flickered and centred at his current location. Just as he was clipping the phone into the dashboard cradle, the better to see it while he drove, a message displayed on the screen, 'No network'.

'Great!' he said, bitterly. 'But still no surprise, I suppose, here in the back of beyond.'

It was as he traced the correct route to his destination that he saw something in the pattern of waterways that put a question-mark in his mind. He then looked at the two marks he had drawn on the map given him by the concert organiser. It didn't make sense that the plan's success would be allowed to be dependent on chance.

Lord Alland had decided where the alternative site must be, but if that meant the concert had been expected to end up at the alternative site all along then it presumed an uncanny faith in the weather in washing out the first site. How could he be certain that the first site would be washed out? And what could have been his motive for introducing such a dangerous complication to the success of his plan?

Black began to believe he was off the track in this line of thought as he simply couldn't allow that Alland would have jeopardized his plan in such a way. There was only one other answer; both the first and second sites must be on the same river. Quickly he traced through the water system but it was obvious almost immediately that the two sites were on different tributaries. Then he had another idea and traced the blue lines back up-country to the dam complex and it was here that he met with success.

The water system was like an inverted tree on the map, each branch leading ultimately to a broader line and ultimately to their own, common source. At first he couldn't believe his eyes. Then, when he had confirmed the truth, he began to feel the dread of knowing he had made a bad mistake. He had sent Davies and his men to the wrong dams; both the first and the alternate concert sites were on tributaries that emanated from the same source, Freshwater Reservoir.

He was tempted at that moment to turn round and find a telephone to contact Davies and change the search area. Then he thought of the time and how long it would take to organise the movement of so many men who might already be deployed on foot at the two locations. Besides, the feeling of dread had begun to be replaced by excitement and, knowing he was only a short drive from the dam, he was impatient to be there. But his better judgement told him it was risky. He might go straight into trouble and, alone and unarmed, he could be in considerable danger. Then the balance of his thinking altered as he remembered that his suggestion not to search the dam may not have been taken seriously and he might arrive to find the place swarming with police.

Anticipation, the urge to progress, call it what you will, is a great motivator and against this the thought of his going back to Davies could not compete. So Black started the car and continued along the road to Freshwater Reservoir, and hoped that Davies had included the dam in his search after all.

Whether he really expected this to happen was difficult for Black to say for in his tiredness he was beginning to imagine that all things were possible. He could also allow in his present state of mind that all things were impossible. It was in acknowledgement of the fact that the latter might be the case that he drove no closer than a mile from the dam before turning the car into a depression out of view from the road and then further draining his physical resources by plodding the rest of the way on foot.

But the reality of the situation hit him as he breasted the last hill before the dam and slowly walked down towards the dam. Look as he may at the scene below he could not detect even the slightest evidence to dispute the fact he was completely alone.

In a way Black felt this was a relief for if he was alone it meant he could rest. He would wait. This was the target without a doubt so he would wait for Alland's men to arrive, hopefully after Davies's men had. Without pause he went out along the catwalk and into the valve-house.

His Immediate reaction on entering was that he could smell burning. He thought this odd but when he found a collection of charred twigs in a corner he understood what had happened.

His mind was still whirring away, despite his fatigue, and he could imagine the plight of hill-walkers caught out in the near blizzard of the morning and forced to seek refuge in the valve-house. But his curiosity still wasn't satisfied. There was something about the burning smell that didn't quite match that of burning wood. It was as if steel had burned, which didn't make any sense at all to Black. Slowly he made a search to discover the cause, looking around the two levels that weren't flooded and even rooting around in the cold grate.

Then he gave up on the problem. He was tired and he needed sleep badly. He felt he would have due warning of any arrivals and so he searched for somewhere to sit that wasn't wet. This wasn't an easy task because the water level on the floor had risen so much that it was now ankle-deep and even the remnants of the fire, raised on bricks above the waterline, were being lapped by the waves as he moved around. But finally he managed to wedge himself in a corner above the waterline and had hardly laid back his head against the dripping wall before he was plummeting down into slumber.

Chapter Thirteen

Black didn't identify in the first few seconds of consciousness just what it was that had wakened him. Indeed, for a while he wasn't even aware where he was and it was with the deepest regret that he managed to wrench himself from relapsing into slumber.

Then he heard the noise again. The slamming of a door, a car door. At this he groggily stumbled to his feet and moved closer to the entrance. He could now hear voices, too: a man's and a woman's. Then he was at the door-way and peering around the jamb more from idle curiosity borne of interrupted sleep than any calculated assessment of the situation.

At first, he looked directly along the catwalk to the causeway on top of the dam but could see nothing that fitted in with what he had heard. Next, he traversed his gaze along the parapet in the direction he had come and woke up with a jerk. Right at the end of the dam, where the water-line could be reached down a short shingle beach, were two people: Alland and Katherine Ross. On the causeway behind them stood a Range Rover and, as Black watched over the next few seconds, they moved several times between the vehicle and a small boat that was just out of the water and lying lop-sided on the shingle.

Of the two, Alland seemed the more active, with the girl just standing out of the way and wearing an unhappy expression. Cautiously Black looked around and out onto the reservoir but could see nothing by way of a potential destination for Alland and the boat. Then it struck him that the drums were hardly likely to be visible and how best to hide them but by sinking them at the bottom of the reservoir.

At this thought, Black remembered the presence of the anglers early in the morning on the reservoir and he now knew that the two men who had visited them at the shooting-box where the same people, and that they had been doing something to the drums when he and the girl had arrived.

Black made up his mind to stop Alland going out. It came back to him that he had been in mine disposal during the war and would know quite a lot about explosives. If he were allowed to get out to where the drums where it could only be to prime some kind of detonator to go off at midnight.

But there was the problem of the girl. If Alland were to see him approach he could grab her and use her as hostage to assure his non-interference. He would have to go carefully and possibly warn her before he lunged for Alland.

With this simple plan decided upon, Black waited for a moment when their backs were turned to him before quickly but silently running along the cat-walk to the concealing bulk of the parapet beyond. At the parapet he looked discreetly at the pair again but they appeared not to have noticed anything amiss. Then came the easy part for the parapet would give continuous cover until he got quite close to the Range Rover, where he could walk round to a position only a few feet from where they stood. Once again luck was with him and for all the time he was running crouched below the parapet they didn't once come into view.

At the Range Rover he paused for a few moments to get his breath back and to allow the pain to subside in his chest that had begun when he had been forced to adopt the crouched running posture. Then he tried to catch the girl's eye without warning Alland.

Twice he came close to detection by Alland before the girl at last caught sight of him. His gestured instruction to silence, a finger placed against his lips, failed to obtain the correct response, however, for she took a deep breath and cried excitedly, 'Uncle Timmie! It's Mr Black.'

Even though he was something over sixty Alland was no slouch physically for immediately he dragged a hand-gun from somewhere about his person and trained it unfalteringly on Black.

'Once upon a time it was 'David',' moaned Black, disgusted at the outcome of his plan.

Alland crossed the few feet of shingle between them. 'Good girl, Kathy. Get me the rope from the car.'

As the girl did as he was bid, Alland spoke again, loudly enough for the girl to hear and it was obvious to Black that she was the intended recipient of what was said. 'So you're the scoundrel masquerading as David Black. I've known David for a long time now. Know a lot about his work, too. I also know that you are not he.'

'You're insane,' was all Black cared to say but he felt he had to say something as the girl was watching him closely.

But Alland wasn't finished and, while the girl carried out his next instruction and tied him up, Black listened to a tale of pure fantasy which made him out to be the villain of the piece instead of Alland. And as the girl didn't throw this out with contempt Black suspected Alland must have spent the time since picking her up indoctrinating her to his version of the story.

In a way Black was relieved at this for if she was the victim of subterfuge, borne out by her obvious confusion and the fact that Alland couldn't possibly have sold her the idea if he had let her see his blitzed house, it meant she could be persuaded back to the truth.

'But we got wise to you, Mr Whatever-your-name-is,' continued Alland. We knew you were on your way to the dam to prime the explosives so I'm going out to make sure you haven't. You see, I too have picked up a few things about radio-controlled bombs along the way.'

'Radio-controlled bombs?' said Black, unable to conceal his interest.

Alland's confident expression never wavered even under the searching glance of the girl. 'Very good,' he said slowly. 'For a moment it sounded as if you really didn't know what was planted in the water.'

Then he turned to the girl. 'As I told you, Kathy. A consummate actor.'

But the girl wasn't convinced. 'Are you positive, Uncle?' she asked, her voice the reflection of tortured thoughts.

'You've trusted my judgement all these years, dear, haven't you?' he answered with a fatherly tenderness.

The girl nodded.

'Then you've no reason to doubt me now.'

Without waiting for any comment on this Alland pushed Black to the ground and stepped back to hand the girl his gun. Then he checked Black's bonds carefully. As he stood up again, he said, 'Now remember, Kathy. This man is extremely dangerous. While I'm defusing the bomb I want you to watch him very carefully. If he so much as moves you must shoot him. Aim for a leg if you have time but if not the biggest target is his chest...,'

'All right! All right!' she cried, very close to tears, which seemed already to have made her eyes red. 'I'll do it Uncle Timmie, just get back as soon as you can.'

Alland patted her arm and Black was surprised to see a look of sadness in his face, which he managed to hide from the girl. 'Good girl,' he said. 'I wouldn't ask you to do this but I have to go out there and I can't be in two places at one time.'

Katherine nodded.

With that, he turned for the boat and with little delay was buzzing his way out on the placid water, the tiny outboard motor throwing up a pall of smoke as Alland forced it on at maximum revolutions.

Back on shore Black spoke urgently. 'Hurry up. Katherine. Untie me. We've got to stop him, he's mad.' Then, in order to help her he sat up, turning his back on her to offer up his bound hands.

'Another move and I promise you I will shoot,' was her response and Black watched as she fought to control the shaking hands that aimed the gun at his torso.

'Don't you see, he's ill. He needs attention,' implored Black, five minutes later, his head buzzing and the sweat beading on his forehead. He had tried every means of persuasion, but until a few seconds ago when the weight had forced her to lower the gun she had shown no sign of response. However, now that the gun wasn't aimed at his chest it did allow him to resume something like normal breathing.

He had reminded her of his liaison with the authorities, the Chairman, the police, the paediatrician and the toxicologist. Of his talking with all the computer authorities. He had invited her to look in his wallet, anything to prove his *bone fides* but to no avail, it seemed.

He hadn't brought up the subject of their liaison: there was no saying what her reaction might be to that. It was best he did no more than refer to it in passing. That was the safest way, he felt sure, and perhaps he might then stay-alive long enough to change her allegiance.

It was a battle of wills, he knew. Of his and Alland's, with the girl as an emotionally-battered referee. As he continued talking, keeping up the pressure to overwhelm the girl with the weighty logic of the truth, he began to see first recognition and then interest in her eyes, and he felt the beginnings of a glimmer of hope.

Still he persisted, until now after tight-packed minutes of continuous battering at an emotional block, she was responding to his meaning - if still stubbornly resisting his story. Now, like Black, her conversation was punctuated with very frequent glances at the small dot out on the reservoir that was Alland. They both knew he must return soon. But unlike Black she didn't feel the urgency of the situation, and therefore couldn't realise that if Alland returned and Black wasn't free he could very soon be a dead man and there would be a few thousand more dead after midnight.

Suddenly, unable to see his watch, he asked her for the time. 'Quarter-to-six,' she answered, but although her tortured mind was distracted there was a glint of curiosity in her eyes. 'Why?'

Black didn't immediately respond. 'Six hours,' he said, almost a whisper. Then he looked up at the girl. 'I've just been told that thousands of people have only hours to live. Not only that, but by someone who is helping to bring it about!'

'I'm not! We're not. It's you,' she gasped.

'When will you believe me!' cried Black, the frustration of not being able to make her understand finally getting to him. Out on the water he saw Alland's frame turn towards them in the stationary boat. 'I visited Highfields Hall an hour ago and guess what I found? Don't bother, I'll tell you.'

He told her. 'What's more I'll bet your uncle spent the whole of the time since he picked you up selling his side of the story. And what's more you didn't go near the house.'

'We did spend a long time in the Range-Rover but he said it wasn't safe to go back to the house.'

'I told you. They've stripped it bare. And that means Hasker and the rest of his staff are in on it.'

'Hasker? He left and then came back in a land-rover,' she said, almost in a trance. But not for long because across the water came the stutter of the outboard as Allan began to return. At the sound Black's heart-rate took a leap and he knew only seconds separated him from the total loss of any way of stopping disaster.

'Does this all strike you as the normal behaviour of law-abiding citizens?' Striving to keep his voice just short of hysterical. 'And if your Uncle is on the side of the angels, why aren't we surrounded by police?'

The girl didn't answer. Black watched her closely, noting almost dispassionately the outward signs of the struggle within her. At one moment she looked out at the boat, the next at Black. It was then that Black knew he had only one chance.

'Untie me, Katherine,' he urged. 'For the sake of several thousand people, untie me?'

Something in Katherine Ross snapped then and she broke out of her indecision. The boat was only three hundred yards out on the water now and as she quickly stooped to untie Black's bonds they heard Alland's voice, an almost animal quality in the anguished shout. 'No, Katherine. No!'

The knots the girl had tied could not be identified by consultation of any manual on the subject. She had not dealt with the problem in any scientific or logical way and therefore when it came to untying the knots it was a tedious chore. As she fought with them Black encouraged her, as much to stop her hearing Alland's voice as to press her on faster.

So slow was her work however that he still felt trussed like a turkey as he watched Alland prepare to ram the bows of the boat up on to the shingle. And Black's hopes began to sink again as he saw that the girl appeared to be making no headway whatsoever. He could only wait.

Then an arm came free from the lashings and the hope this brought had Black scrabbling with numbed fingers at the ropes around his legs. But at the same time as he undid the first of what seemed a maze of knots down there he saw that

Alland was ashore and trying to run up the bank, impeded a little by the regressive effect of the soft shingle. Then Black's other arm was free.

'The gun, Katherine,' prompted Black. 'Give me the gun.'

'No!' she cried, picking up the gun and moving backwards away from him towards the Range Rover. And in her eyes was the frightened indecision she had shown when weighing the merits of the two men's stories just minutes ago.

Seeing this Alland altered course for the girl, passing several feet to the side of Black. But he hadn't realised that the still supine figure had both arms free, coiled as he still was in the long rope. He also didn't see Black spring from the ground in a standing rugby tackle. And it was far too late for him to do anything as Black wrapped his arms around his legs, except fall heavily to the ground.

Swiftly Black shrugged off the last of his bonds and rose to his feet. However, there was no need to rush now for the fall had winded Alland and he was only just beginning to force himself to a sitting position. Alland and Black were now equidistant from the startled girl although Black had the advantage by being on his feet. Quickly he advanced upon the girl, holding out his hand. 'Give me the gun, Katherine. It's all over.'

At that the girl's shoulders sagged and she lowered the gun.

'No, Katherine,' cried Alland, a pitiful quality about his plea. 'Please, I beg you don't give him the gun.'

The outburst stopped both of them in their tracks and for a moment the girl hesitated.

Then Black turned to Alland as he heard himself addressed. 'Please, Mr Black,' he uttered. 'If you would spare my wife's life, don't take the gun.'

'What?' cried Black, incredulous. But as the remark sank in he felt as if he had just been handed the answer to a troublesome problem. Instead of continuing in the same voice he thought a moment before saying, mildly, 'Of course, your wife has been kidnapped.'

'Kidnapped?' cried the girl, but she had no time to expand on this because Alland was now talking.

'Not only that. Mr Black. If I don't soon appear to be back in charge of the situation here she won't be the only one to die. You see, there is a rifle trained on us right at this moment.'

Chapter Fourteen

'With age one loses the stomach for action,' confessed Alland. They were in the valve-house now, Alland having ushered Black there ostensibly against his will. Behind him had come the girl carrying the rope.

Black moved over to a window. 'Do you know where our sniper is located?' he asked, an urgency in his voice. At the same time as he spoke he moved over to one of the broken windows and began peering at a landscape which was beginning to fade with the onset of dusk.

'I've no idea,' replied Alland nervously, following Black's lead and choosing to look out through the doorway. 'They left before us. But you can be sure he is somewhere on the high ground.'

'How many are there?

'Three. Hasker, Robson and Barrowmans. Barrowmans is the sniper.' he explained. 'Not a very good one but who needs to be with a telescopic sight.'

'If he set it up correctly,' interjected Black. Then he turned his attention from the landscape to look at Alland. 'Robson and Barrowmans. Big and little chap?'

'That's them. And nasty work, too.'

Black glanced quickly to the girl. 'You all right?'

The girl nodded but said nothing, avoiding looking either of the two men in the eye.

There were a lot of questions Black wanted to ask both Alland and the girl but he hadn't the patience for a long-winded history of why Alland had gone bad. However, there were points that required clarification if he was to establish whether the man and the girl could be part of his plan to get out of their present predicament.

'Katherine,' he called. 'Keep a lookout at the door and tell me the moment you see anything approach the causeway. I have a few questions I want to ask your uncle.'

Hurriedly the girl splashed her way over to the doorway.

'Now let's make this quick,' instructed Black. 'Hasker is the ring-leader, right?'

'Right,' returned Alland. 'I found out just thirty hours ago that he had come to my home under false pretences. I gave him a job out of recognition of the fact that we had served in the same regiment in the late sixties. Didn't realise that in the past two years he was just using me. He had this planned long before he came to me...'

Black held up his hand. 'I don't need a blow-by-blow alibi. Just tell me what you think is his motive behind all this.'

Alland was angry at Black's manner but he didn't show it in his reply. 'He's getting even, or so he says. He once had a to-do with an official who he claimed had been allowing illegal dumping of toxic wastes. Hasker complained by the normal means and with an extremely strong case, but the result was a white-wash anyway.'

'Which made Hasker a little mad,' put in Black.

'More than that, it seems. It ended with him being put in prison when the police found out he was burning down chemical plants.

'So he has a record?'

'Yes, but all his crimes were under an assumed name: Anderson. That's why I didn't get any information about his recent past through references.'

'Anderson,' said Black, trying to find some significance in the name. Then a thought occurred to him. 'Big A?'

Alland nodded. 'That's what his two cronies call him, yes.'

'Why did he come to you?'

'Rather obvious, really. He knew me from the services, as I've said, and also heard that I was something of an antipollution campaigner. No doubt the fact that I knew a lot of contacts and had the run of this land had something to do with it.'

'So our Mr Hasker came along to you for a job - which you gave him - and bided his time for something really promising to come along.'

Alland nodded. 'That was Henshaw. A tragedy.' Lord Alland looked old now, the anxiety furrowing every wrinkle on his face just a little deeper. 'He came to me one evening with the story that Garrison were producing a high-yield TCP, the high-yield being TCDD. No doubt you'll know about such things in your profession.'

'Go on,' urged Black.

'Well, I tied it in with a larger operation I had been monitoring for some time. I realise now I was shooting in the dark, of course. The incident that poisoned those poor children was organised as a harmless demonstration meant to point to pollution in the area. It was I who added the telephone call asking for inquiries to be directed to Arrowsmith.'

'It was Arrowsmith who brought me in on the case,' said Black. 'He must have a great deal of respect for you. He tried his best to divert my inquiries away from you.'

'It wouldn't be the first mistake I made in this affair. My wife was another. If I hadn't been so preoccupied with fighting the shadows of big-time polluters I might have seen what was going on behind my back.'

'Why didn't you go to the police - or contact me?'

Alland smiled a grim smile. 'You've got to be in the same predicament as I was before you can answer that.'

'But surely anything was better than this,' Black waved his arms around to indicate their present location.

'There was the matter of me, as well,' said the girl, quietly.

Alland seemed surprised at her words but although he was going to say something, the girl shook her head to stop him. 'He was trying to protect me, Mr Black. I realise that now. The only reason he told me about the Circle and his part in it was so that I would volunteer to spy for him at the inn.' She turned to face Alland. 'I don't know how you manipulated me into suggesting it, but I've no doubt you did. And the reason behind it was to get me away from the house and Hasker, in the only way Hasker would likely allow.'

Alland said nothing.

'And from then on you passed information on my movements to Hasker,' added Black, 'thinking they would go to your uncle.'

It was the girl's turn to remain silent but her expression said enough to confirm Black's belief.

But Black was not assuaged. 'All very noble. I'm sure!' he cried. 'But no damned use whatsoever to the thousands of people who are facing death in just a few hours from now!'

Alland's eyes were momentarily defiant. 'You don't think I could stand-by and let that happen do you?'

Black was angry now. 'What else am I to believe?'

'That I went out there,' his arm pointed to the reservoir,' to defuse the bomb. It took me twenty-four hours to persuade Hasker that it needed checking and that I should do it.' Alland's voice was raised as he spoke, but then he paused before adding, 'I fully realise how dangerous the situation is but how would you have played it in the same circumstances?'

Black couldn't answer the question, neither would he bother trying as it was academic now.

Then he turned to Alland. Something in the man's tone had formed a question-mark in Black's brain. It was as if Alland had meant to say something else but changed his mind at the last moment. Alland was afraid. Black knew, and this fear was driving him under.

This worried Black like nothing else at that moment for he realised that if they were to carry out the plan he had formed in his mind he needed Lord Alland's intelligent cooperation. The man needed hope. It was time for him to stretch truth and supply that hope. 'Lord Alland, I know where your wife is.'

Alland's head came up at that. 'Where?' he said, urgently.

'She is quite safe and in a room at the *George*. Inspector Davies should be there by now and I think Appleton might just have cracked under the strain and told him about her presence.'

Alland's eyes lit up at that.

So did the girl's. 'The eccentric old lady! Of course, I never saw her. I didn't think.'

Black decided it was time to moderate their heightening emotions. He was only too aware that they were being watched by Hasker and his men, and the longer they stayed in the valve-house the deeper would be Hasker's suspicions. This meant he would soon be considering action, like paying a visit to either the reservoir or the valve-house.

'But what must concern us now,' he said sternly, 'is how we deal with our predicament.' That brought silent interest.

'As I see it there is only one thing we can do,' he continued. 'We must wait here and stop Hasker and his men from getting out onto the reservoir in that boat. It means building any kind of barricade for protection and it also means using that handgun to hold off a rifle and possibly other weapons for anything up to twenty-four hours - until the police stumble across us.'

'That long? We saw lots of police around on the way up here,' said the girl. 'The only reason we got through the cordon at all was because uncle owns the land and is so well known anyway.'

'There were a lot of policemen around,' corrected Black, not relishing what he was saying. 'Until I sent them the wrong way!'

Neither of the two listeners commented on this and for a moment this irritated Black. 'Well?' he asked, inviting comment.

Alland gave a grim smile. 'He who is without sin…'

Black tried to smile too but it didn't work. 'We'll just have to sit it out and hope we can hold off until they arrive. Now let's get to work on that barricade.'

'It isn't quite as simple as that,' announced Lord Alland.

Black stopped in his watery tracks and turned back to face Alland, sensing something of foreboding in Alland's tone. 'How do you mean?'

'The bomb is primed.'

Black didn't understand. 'But you went out there. You just said you defused the bomb.'

' I didn't have time before I had to get back to try and stop Kathy setting you free,' was Alland's anguished reply. 'Remember, I knew you were under constant surveillance by a gun-man who would have no compunction in shooting both of you. I just left the stuff on the surface and headed back for the shore.'

For a moment there was complete silence. Black, for his part, was shattered by the news. It seemed they were in an impossible situation.

But with the grim determination never to give in, which was almost his trade-mark, Black surfaced above the problem to think again in his usual rational way. 'So we have a bomb out there which might go off at any time, or just at midnight when the deadline is reached. Whatever else is certain, we can be sure that if we make any attempt to approach them they will press the button. Am I right, Lord Alland?'

Alland nodded.

'Which means the only thing we can do is think of ourselves and stay here until reinforcements arrive, even if that happens to be after they push the button to start the poison going down river to those poor unsuspecting people.'

Again there was a moments silence, both Alland and the girl concentrating their attention on Black's every word, every movement. Then Black's eyes gleamed briefly. 'But if they blow the explosive and none of the poison gets out of the reservoir we are back to our original situation.'

'I don't follow,' said Alland.

'The dam. It's just a large scale tap. If we shut the valves, which allow water to pass through the dam, we can contain the poison to this reservoir. A hell of a disaster in any case, what with the effect on the flora and fauna and the fact that this whole area will have to be sealed off, but at least it contains the danger to some extent.'

'I see.'

'Then let's get cracking,' urged Black. 'They may decide to blow the explosive early.'

With that they attacked the valves in the corner, all three straining in unison at each one of the four hand-wheels. But not one of the four budged by even a millimetre. 'I can't understand it,' ' said Black, panting from his exertions. 'I managed to move one of these on my own this morning. Not much, but a little bit, nevertheless.'

Then he remembered the smell of burning and his odd idea that it smelled of steel. 'Welding!' he cried, to the utter amazement of the other two. Then he began to claw frantically at the grimy spindle of the nearest hand-wheel. It took only two seconds to expose an area of brighter metal a half-inch square that was a metal bond between the screw and casing of the valve. 'They've welded the bloody hand-wheels. That was why they lit a fire, to try to disguise it! '

'Why would they do that?' asked the girl, a frown joining the rest of the expression on her face.

'Don't you see?' cried Black, irritated by her lack of understanding. 'They've welded the hand-wheels open so that we cannot stop the poison leaving the reservoir once they detonate the charge...'

He had been about to expand on this but a new thought had emerged which made him freeze. 'Oh, Christ!' he yelled. 'That is only part of the reason. They screwed the hand-wheels down first. They gauged the outflow to below the rate at which the dam is filling and welded the valves open to that point. They want the reservoir to roll-over the dam.'

'Breach the dam? That's absurd,' said Alland.

'Not at all! We've just had a period of exceptionally wet weather. The hills must be water-logged. That water is coming into this reservoir all the time and the level is already high. They may not have to blow the drums at all, the water-could do it for them: roll-over the dam, broach the drums in the ensuing maelstrom and you not only have a highly poisonous liquid descending on everyone in the valley, you have several million gallons in a tidal wave. It could make the addition of poison a far too subtle ingredient, the force would devastate anything in its path.'

Black shook his head angrily, 'You said Hasker had been thinking this thing out for over two years. How the hell are we supposed to compete with that given only hours?' It was a question none of them could answer, and none tried.

'What can we do?' the girl was trying not to be hysterical but it wasn't working very well, On the other hand Alland seemed to have changed. His back seemed a little straighter and he had a look in his eyes that worried Black,

But Black gave the girl an answer. 'I honestly don't know. We can't stay here, that's for certain.' Then he sighed deeply before continuing, striving to get his thoughts together. 'We now have two problems; stopping them blowing the drums and saving the dam from bursting. And we can't stop the second without neutralizing Hasker's sniper.'

'That makes three tasks,' corrected Alland. 'I assume the most immediate problem is that of defusing the bomb?'

Black nodded. 'That would seem the case. The dam might go at any time. Who knows how stable such a structure is after so many years of neglect.' Black gave no edge to the latter remark knowing that it would serve no purpose to thrust the lack of maintenance at an already worried Lord Alland. He would have plenty of time to air recriminations if they got out of this mess. And at that moment it was a very big *if*. 'I would have said Hasker was the first objective but not with only a hand-gun as artillery.'

By now Black understood the only practical scheme available to them, and one without any ending; just the first phase of a plan. If it worked they might move on to the next stage. But he also knew it was too much to expect. He shrugged, and both the girl and Lord Alland saw it as a gesture of despair.

Then Black found out just what it was that had put the gleam back in Alland's eye and knew that both of them were thinking on the same lines.

'I have a plan,' announced Lord Alland.

Although it would be Alland who was most exposed to danger both Black and the girl had a taste of it on their way back to the Range Rover. Black was tied-up again but his bonds were so arranged that he had merely to open his hand for the rope to fall off him. Behind him Lord Alland prodded him along the way with the snout of the gun until they arrived at their destination whereupon he wrapped the rope several times around Black's legs. In the process the gun disappeared from view although it appeared from Alland's rummaging inside his coat that he had placed it there. Then with much theatrical gesticulation, meant solely for the attention of their hidden observers, Alland ran down the shingle and set off in the boat.

In an attempt to reassure the watching Hasker against a repetition of the previous incident out on the causeway. Black had been placed at one end of the Range Rover while the girl sat at the other. This arrangement also gave them some measure of comfort because one of them must be screened from the gun-man's view whatever his vantage. Even though it was a fifty-fifty chance, they were both instinctively grateful for even that; out on the reservoir Alland had no means of escape whatsoever.

The whole feasibility of Alland's plan rested on the fact that because he had been in the middle of dealing with the explosives when he had seen what was happening on shore, he had had to leave with the electrical box of tricks still on the surface and its water-proof container open to the elements.

Exposed as they were the explosives package could only arouse suspicion of any searchers who visited the reservoir and therefore constituted an embarrassment to Hasker's intended plan to release the chemical at midnight. But with the box open on the surface Alland hoped the one thought which dominated all others in Hasker's cunning mind was whether the explosives were primed or not?

It was upon this question that the trio staked the success of their plan. Even though they were desperate, knowing full well their survival depended upon it, it had been the plan's feasibility which had given them the courage to leave the valve-house in the first place. After all, there was only one way Hasker could find out if the explosive was primed without getting word from Alland, or seeing himself, and that was by pressing the button. And though it was realised Hasker wouldn't hesitate to press the button prematurely if he suspected anything was wrong, they also believed he wouldn't do it without good reason because the noise of the explosion would carry to the ears of the men deployed on the other dams, and throw away all chance of the Bill being considered when it was learned that the poison had been deployed.

Their plan was simple, it was hoped that Hasker would believe Alland had taken them to the valve-house to sort them out and then re-emerged to finish the job. Then Alland would defuse the explosive and allow the drums to sink to the bottom again, disconnecting the short almost invisible radio-aerial as absolute insurance against detonation.

Both Black and the girl knew it was risky and their tenseness was demonstrated by the fact that they didn't speak once until Alland had stopped the boat and leaned over the side to resume work on the explosives. Then, as had been arranged, the girl passed this information to Black in an unnecessarily low voice. Black for his part clenched and unclenched his hands in order that they shouldn't become numb and debilitate his use of the gun that Alland had so deftly slipped inside his jacket.

'See any movement anywhere?' he asked, aware that if he did get a chance to use the gun the ranges involved would most probably make it as effective as throwing a balloon in gale force winds. He could only hope that they would be close-by, very close, no more than thirty yards and even that was pushing it. But at least he knew he had hit things at that range before.

'Nothing. I can't see any sign of them,' responded the girl.

'You might get a reflection or something so keep looking,' he instructed and then got back to what was taking most of his concentration. 'Come on, Alland,' he breathed quietly. 'Defuse the thing and get out of there.'

He didn't concentrate on it for much longer however because his attention was diverted by the girl. 'He's fallen!' she called and they both heard the report of a gun being fired. Then the girl screamed. 'He's dead! They've killed him!' she cried.

Then she shut up as Black, who had quickly sprung to his feet, lunged for her and dragged her down low. 'Where did the shot come from?' he demanded.

'I don't know,' mumbled the girl, terrified.

Then she cowered beneath Black's covering form as they heard two slamming noises in quick succession and felt the vibration through the metal skin of the vehicle. Then came the two reports.

In one brief surveying glance Black looked around the gleaming panels of the Range Rover. 'They must be over the other side,' he said. 'There are no holes on this side of the car.' With that he peeped over the bonnet, keeping his head as low as he could. Then he saw a flash from the trees high-up on the right hand bank of the reservoir. And then another.

The boat, with Alland's form just visible slumped inside, had now drifted from its previous position and Black wondered for all of a second whether Alland had managed to defuse the explosive. Then he saw the spurts of water where the boat had once been and Black's spirits rose.

'He must have done it!' he cried, not really addressing the girl but unable to contain his elation. 'They're trying to hit the drums with rifle-fire. And they haven't a chance if the drums are on their way to the bottom again.'

But then there came a very loud explosion that saw Black fall back behind the bulk of the vehicle as fast as his reflexes would allow while the girl cringed with her eyes tight-shut on the ground. Black saw her and thought for a moment she'd been hit. Quickly he stooped over her. 'Are you all right, Katherine?'

The girl nodded without opening her eyes. 'What's happening?'

Black sighed with relief at her well-being but he frowned when he realised just what the explosion meant. 'It looks like they detonated the explosion with rifle-fire. Which means they've broached the drums and released the chemical.'

Then Black ducked as he heard more gunfire, thinking that they were firing at him. But when he didn't hear any impact noises he quickly darted a glance over the bonnet again.

The scene on the reservoir puzzled him. As the gunfire continued he saw more spurts of water rising in the same place as before. The boat was now well away, seemingly undamaged and drifting towards the dam. For a few seconds Black tried to figure out what was going on. If they had hit the explosives and blown up the drums surely there was no point still firing at the same spot.

After his short-lived elation of a few moments earlier he was not keen to leap to conclusions a second time. But even so it now looked as if they had detonated the explosive but failed to rupture the drums. Then he wondered how this could have happened. What if the reason they had shot at Alland in the first place hadn't been because he had defused the explosive but because in addition he had cut the explosive away and let it drift free? That would fit. What was more, no amount of rifle-fire was likely to puncture the drums because they must already be quite some distance below the surface of the water.

But he didn't have time to relish his assumptions because the Range Rover became the target for a fusillade of shots which kept him and the girl pinned down behind the vehicle.

It was difficult for Black to judge but he got the feeling that the gun-man's aim got progressively worse rather than better and he heard the ricochets off the concrete many feet away from the vehicle.

After a few seconds, which seemed an eternity, the firing suddenly ceased. For a few seconds more Black stayed as he was but then he raised himself to a crouched position and lifted the gun as well as the least possible amount of his head above the bonnet again.

But he didn't see anything there at first because his attention was diverted by a movement to his right. There was a blue land-rover bouncing down the track at speed. Then it began the turn that would bring it onto the causeway. From the window protruded the long snout of a rifle which rested on the frame behind the driver's seat.

It was aimed at Black.

Chapter Fifteen

'What are you doing?' cried the girl, her face white with fear.

Black had swiftly drawn the gun and now rested it along the bonnet of the Range Rover. 'The boat!' he barked. 'They're after the boat!'

Black had realised immediately what was in Hasker's mind. They had wanted Black and the girl pinned down while the land-rover reduced the range between them. The boat was now little more than twenty yards out on the water, drifting slowly but surely towards the dam and Black knew that Hasker wanted to use it to get out to the drums. Black also knew that the boat was within range of his hand-gun and he had no intention of letting it fall into Hasker's hands. He gambled that with the land-rover being a moving platform it would put the sniper off his aim.

As carefully as he could in the rushed moment Black levelled the sights on the petrol tank of the outboard motor and began to squeeze the trigger.

'No!' yelled the girl, pushing Black's arm sufficiently off aim to send the shot well wide and harmlessly into the reservoir. 'He's alive! I saw him move!'

Black ignored her words, roughly pushing her to one side and very conscious that he would be very lucky to get a second shot. The girl was wrong, Alland was dead.

He could see the approaching land-rover out of the corner of his eye as he quickly took aim for a second time. And again he began to squeeze.

Then he saw what the girl had seen. It was a movement too easy to miss, just the slight arching of the spine as if Alland were taking a deep breath in his sleep.

In the second that Black hesitated he realised he was too late, for the land-rover had now stopped; the rifle trained unerringly on him.

Very slowly he stood up, casting his arms wide before the constant gaze of the gun-man who stood just twenty yards away. He recognized the man then, seeing the bigger of the two men he had felled outside the shooting-box and knew he could expect no mercy from that quarter. In submission he began slowly to open his right hand as he prepared to drop the gun to the ground.

Suddenly the gun-man stiffened and so did Black as he anticipated the thud of the bullet that would see his demise. Then he saw the gun-man swivel his aim out on the reservoir and once again Black saw something out of the corner of his eye, his left this time, as he discerned the drunken form of Alland striving to stand in the boat.

Without hesitation, the gun was back firmly in Black's palm and traversing to take aim on the gun-man. He didn't hesitate now and after swiftly checking the swing of the gun with his left palm he squeezed the trigger.

Simultaneously the gun-man fired and then took off backwards as the bullet Black had fired jerked his head back viciously. To his left Black glimpsed Alland, seeing him spin like a rag doll before landing half-in-and half out of the boat.

Before the last echo had faded Black was aware that the girl was running to the parapet. He himself was running, but towards the land-rover.

He had covered perhaps ten yards before he saw the figure of the little man jump into view. Black gave him no chance this time for with a running shot he collapsed the figure before he had completed the back-swing of the knife whose blade was intended for him.

When he got to the land-rover it was to find only one other occupant, Hasker. The man offered no resistance whatsoever, which was a shame as Black was in the mood to clout him very hard. As it was he merely dragged him from the vehicle, found some cord and trussed him up so tightly that it was surprising he could still breath. Then he pushed him to the ground.

It required only a cursory glance at the other two to see they were both dead and so he didn't waste time in getting over to the parapet and to the spot where the girl was now struggling to support Alland.

'Will he be all right?' she asked, as he relieved her of the load.

Black dragged Alland's heavy frame onto the concrete and then checked his injuries. There were two wounds. One, a bullet hole, passed through the fleshy part of his right arm and Black suspected it had been this that had caused him to do his pirouette moments before. Like most bullet holes, it had a small entry point but had ended as a crater on the other side, culminating in the loss of a lot of blood. 'Hold your hand on there,' he instructed, guiding her hand to a pressure point.

The other wound was on the head. Alland had spoken of Barrowman's inaccurate shooting but the gun-man couldn't have got closer than he had with this shot. The wound was a large gash where the bullet had forced a ragged furrow-through his scalp to reveal the whiteness of his skull beneath. But like a lot of head wounds it looked infinitely worse than it was.

'He'll live,' proclaimed Black, hoping he was as right as his confidence suggested. Then he turned to the girl. She was looking pretty battered now, and although Black had urgent business elsewhere he sought briefly to lessen her load with a few gentle words and by gently stroking away the tears which came in a gush of sobs. 'He'll be all right. Help is on its way. The shots and the explosion must have been heard in the next valley.'

Then he got to his feet and strode over to Hasker. It was his first study of the man and he could now see little resemblance to the one who had tried to repulse him from Highfields Hall, twenty-four hours ago. Now he could see why

Hasker had effected such a disguise as he had. With his hair combed in a strict conservative style, matched also by his dress, the man bore little resemblance to his former appearance and Black assumed that Hasker's desire not to be linked with his alias of Anderson had been the reason behind his simple but effective change to the attire of a younger man. And cunning too, for Alland would not have seen his army associate for many years and it would therefore have been difficult for him to judge how much Hasker would have aged in the interim.

'Don't for a minute think you've won,' announced Hasker, contemptuously. 'This dam is going to go soon and there is nothing you can do to stop it.'

Black didn't answer but instead walked quickly to the land-rover and peered in the back. It was as he expected. Heaped in the centre of the floor were several pressurized bottles with various tubes and implements around them. It took no more that a glance to identify them, and see that amongst the welding gear was an oxy-acetylene kit. Then without hesitation he ran back to Hasker and dragged him to his feet.

In all the time it took to shove the man towards the land-rover he said nothing. It wasn't until they were at the tail-board that he said, 'You've just one chance to get to a nice comfortable court followed by a nice cosy prison cell. This is it,' He waved to the bottles.

'You're not serious,' accused Hasker, his eyes tinged with the look of fear.

'I'm certainly not laughing,' responded Black. 'You're going to help me drag these bottles to the valve-house and then you are going to un-weld those valves.'

'But there isn't time?' Hasker was excited now, his eyes darting about him for a means of escape; the reflection of a cunning brain in operation. 'I don't know how to operate this stuff.'

Black's tone was patient when he spoke. 'Umpteen years in bomb disposal and you never learned how to use cutting gear? Now I am laughing.' But no trace of mirth reached his face.

Hasker hadn't given up. 'I won't do it. It... it's suicide.'

Black nodded, 'You're probably right. However, you will either help me with this gear and do as I ask or I will tie you to a hand-wheel and leave you there.'

Hasker said nothing.

'All right,' sighed Black. 'I'll do it. You can watch.'

Hasker's eyes widened further. 'You... You sure you know what you're doing?'

'Haven't the same experience as you, of course,' admitted Black fiddling with the array of tubes nearest the tailboard. 'I've only done it once - in a classroom. I seem to remember the instructor wasn't too keen on the state of my handiwork. Never mind, I won't be trying anything technical like undoing the welds you put on there. I'll be going for the casing. Off with its head, as it were.'

'That'll take hours?'

Black seemed to think about this for a moment, 'Yes, several hours. Each. Say twelve hours in all if things go right,' Then he turned swiftly to Hasker. 'D'you think we've enough gas for that long?'

'I'll do it,' said Hasker wearily.

As it was they didn't need to haul the heavy gear themselves for as they began to lift the heavy bottles from the vehicle they heard a noise behind them. In the distance a small, convoy of police vehicles wound its way down the road and soon filed onto the causeway. Then as soon as the first one came to a halt the recognizable figure of Davies leapt out, who, after listening to Black's very brief outline of the situation called four of his men forward to deal with the cutting gear while Black pushed Hasker towards the valve-house.

Fifteen minutes had passed and Black had already had one near mutiny from Hasker by the time Davies joined the two men in the valve-house. The two smaller valves were now wide open but the first of the two storm-sluices had been tricky and thinking he had botched the job Hasker had turned to flee. It had required quick reflexes and a few more threats for Black to send the now sweating and begrimed old man back to his task.

But he had been right, anyway. The first of the two storm-sluices would now require several hours of work to allow its use again. It had taken nerve on the part of both men to allow Hasker the chance of coming good with the second sluice. Now he had almost finished.

'Alland's on his way to hospital,' announced Davies, 'and I sent the girl with him. She didn't want to but I persevered.'

'You mean she wanted to stay here?' responded Black with surprise. He had just finished checking for the third time that the two smaller valves were fully open and now he ducked below the pipe-work to be with Davies.

'Something about you, I gather,' grinned the inspector. 'Still, she pricked up her ears a bit when I mentioned that Lord Alland's wife is safe and well. You knew she was at the inn, didn't you?'

'I had an idea. I take it the other woman was one of Hasker's troupe.'

Davies nodded and then looked around. 'How's it going?'

Black told him about the storm-sluice.

Davies raised an eyebrow. 'Isn't it a little unwise our still being here?'

'A trifle,' murmured Black. 'Why do you think I asked you to clear all your men away? Anyway, if we can get the second storm-sluice open we should have a better chance of saving the dam than at present....' Then Black stopped as he heard voices outside.

Davies saw the question on his face. 'I forgot to tell you, the Chairman's on his way over. This should be him.'

John Arrowsmith might have been on a royal tour for the way he splashed into the valve-house, a smile lighting his face.

Behind him was another man, carrying what looked like a radio over his shoulder,

'Well done, Black,' smiled the Chairman effusively. 'Knew you could do it. We'll have Alland behind bars in no time.'

Black didn't seem interested and so Arrowsmith followed his gaze to the man who had accompanied him. Then his expression changed.

'Mr Rossiter,' he announced.

'I spoke to you on the phone,' explained the man and Black recognized the voice of the reporter he had called earlier. 'Thanks for the story'.

'You haven't got the story yet,' interrupted Black.

'I gave him the background on the way up,' provided the Chairman, 'and then he heard as much as I got from the police up on the causeway just now.'

'You mean about Alland and Hasker?'

'Of course,' answered Arrowsmith, a frown beginning to form on his face.

'There's a lot more than that.' Black looked over to the newspaperman. 'Are you recording this?'

The reporter pressed a switch on a gadget he was carrying. 'I am now.'

In the corner Hasker straightened from his task and quickly closed off the gas to the torch. As he lifted the visor he nodded and Black acknowledged the fact that he had finished in the same way.

It was only then that the Chairman realised it was Hasker. 'What is he doing here?' he asked indignantly, not clear in the structure of his question.

'Waiting for a bus,' offered Black but then shook his head before telling Arrowsmith and the reporter why they were still on the dam when it might disintegrate at any moment.

Of the two newcomers, the Chairman definitely went whitest, his pallor evident even in the gloom of the valve-house now that the illumination from the torch had ceased.

And Hasker had a reaction to Black's brief words too. 'For God's sake let's get this thing open and get out of here,' he cried, already struggling without success to turn the large hand-wheel.

'You'll never do it alone,' said Black, knowing that this was the one that he had barely been able to budge himself when he had first visited the valve-house that morning. 'You need a hand.'

With that Black moved towards Hasker but then veered away to finish up with his back to the wall nearest the door. In the process he had put both hands in his pockets. 'Why don't you give him a hand, Mr Arrowsmith?' he suggested.

The reaction was as he expected. After a brief glance at the struggling Hasker, the Chairman looked quizzically at Black. 'Do you want to give me a hernia?' he said breezily.

Black's face was impassive. 'No. I want you to give our friend Hasker here a hand. You should do it all right. I could just about move it on my own this morning.'

The Chairman couldn't think of an answer to that. Neither did he see fit to carry out the suggestion. Then Davies cleared his throat. 'I don't know what your game is Black, but if it'll get us off this dam I for one won't shirk my share of the load.'

Black shook his head and at the same time withdrew his right hand from his pocket. In *his* hand was the gun and he trained it on Davies. 'I am not playing a game,' said Black calmly. 'But I want both criminals turning that wheel.' He paid no heed to the shocked looks this brought but went on, 'Sort of appropriate; the two men who caused all this trouble taking pains to put it right again.'

The Chairman was obviously mortified but he moved towards Hasker and the wheel. 'You're talking a lot of nonsense, Black. That I must say. I will help open this valve but I promise you will pay for your impudence.'

But as the Chairman got to the wheel Davies began to walk forward to help. 'Back off, Davies,' said Black, waving him back with the gun.'

'Be sensible, man!' cried the inspector. 'The dam might go at any time. The water level is very high. The more there are to help, the quicker it'll be open and we can leave.'

'Feel free to leave now,' responded Black. 'What is to be said here will just have to remain a secret between me, the Chairman and Hasker. Assuming we have time to say it, of course.'

Davies looked at the newspaperman. 'You'd better get out of here.'

'No chance,' was his answer.

'Look, I am telling you to get out of here,' he barked. The newspaperman shrugged. 'You can always carry me, I suppose. But I sense a big story and if you want to get me out of here that is the only way you'll manage it.'

Without any back-up Davies knew his limitations and therefore he turned to Black. 'Don't be bloody stupid,' he shouted but Black said nothing until the inspector then decided to go and help the two men who were making heavy work of it.

'You only get one warning,' said Black and raised the gun so that it was aimed at Davies's head. 'This way you don't even get to hear the story because there is no way in the world you are going to deprive me of this.'

For a few moments, Davies looked down the barrel of the gun. Black was right, he decided, he would like to hear the story too. Then he stepped back and leaned against the wall. 'Once upon a time...'

Black acknowledged the introduction with a nod and then lowered the gun to a more comfortable position, 'Once upon a time,' he repeated, 'a wealthy, titled land-owner with more guts than most, began a campaign over the old-boy network by way of which he hoped to stop his powerful acquaintances poisoning this country with industrial pollution.

'With some it worked. A little blackmail was all that was required to bring them to their moral senses. With one it didn't work, however. This person escaped not only persuasion but also identification because, you see, he had his finger in so many pies that he could bury himself well behind the front men running his enterprises. Then, as they spent time in jail, he continued to prosper.

'But the wealthy landowner didn't give in very easily. He decided that one of his acquaintances had to be the man he couldn't find. He then decided on a larger campaign, a larger operation whereby he would snipe at his contemporaries in the hope of getting a reaction. He only had time to try once before Hasker moved in on him for his own radical gains. But all the same he hit his elusive target first time.'

The large hand-wheel was beginning to turn faster now as the hidden, greased portion of the thread cut down the impeding friction between it and the casing. Soon, Black knew, the valve would be fully open and he would have no legitimate reason to hold back the witnesses. He decided to cut his story to the briefest possible.

'Enter one dashing young man of immaculate credentials,' he continued. 'Me. I had been working until yesterday morning on the very same goal as had our anti-polluter. However, I had been getting to the man's identity in a very slow but methodical fashion. I was only hours behind him.'

Black looked again at the two perspiring men, a little disappointed that their attention had to be shared with their physical task.

'But unfortunately he knew it. Don't ask me how, I don't know. What I do know is that after he had been given reason to believe his contemporary was sniping at him he thought he would kill two birds with one stone by setting me and him against each other. He had me brought in, thereby taking me off the scent for long enough for him to muddy his trail a bit more. Then he made sure I didn't get to his friend until the friend had had enough time to be caught red-handed.'

For a moment-or-so Black reflected silently on whether he had left anything vital out of his story but couldn't think of anything off-hand.

'Didn't you, Mr Arrowsmith?'

Arrowsmith didn't immediately answer but this was due to the effect of physical exertion rather than collecting his thoughts. 'Absolute rubbish,' he cried, mouth wide as he fought to get air to his lungs. Then he stood as both men stopped turning the wheel. The storm-sluice was now fully open.

Black went on. 'You see you made one great error right at the beginning of this incident when you were chairing the emergency meeting of the Area Health Authority. You received a telephone call from our newspaper friend, here, who only a few hours ago told me what he had said to you.

When I discovered that you knew who had called the newspaper, because you recognized the voice described to you by the newspaperman, a few things dropped into place and I knew why you had got me here.'

'I shall sue you for this. Black!' shouted Arrowsmith, defiantly.

'No more or less than I expected,' sighed Black, in response to Arrowsmith's remark. 'Outrage, indignation, whatever. One cannot expect a man, who has wheeled-and-dealed all his life, to give up so easily. No, the immediate reaction could be no other.' Then Black straightened from his leaning position on the wall. 'You need time to think, don't you,' he said, sympathetically.

'I've told you,' panted Arrowsmith, hanging on to the hand-wheel for support, 'you're talking absolute rubbish and placing all our lives in grave danger by keeping us here.'

Black seemed to ignore his remarks. 'Inspector? Would you mind escorting Hasker and our reporter friend to the safety of the road, please?'

For a moment Davies was dumbfounded at Black's words and the fleeting expression he wore. At the time, the Chairman was bent double in an attempt to make life easier on his lungs. It was a calculated risk that Davies would accept Black's intimation to play along, especially as moments ago he was threatening to blow his head off. However, Davies had picked up a story since then that had purported to indicate the Chairman as a

criminal and so he grudgingly agreed to the subterfuge.

'What about the Chairman...er, Mr Arrowsmith?' he asked.

Black stooped to pick up a piece of rope that
had been used to haul the gas-bottles. 'Oh, he isn't
going anywhere,' replied Black calmly, whereupon he moved over to Arrowsmith. 'He's going
to stay here until he decides to tell us the truth. I'll
just tie him to this valve.'

Black lay the gun within very easy reach as he
fiddled with the rope, tying Arrowsmith's hands
to the valve-stem of the storm-sluice.

'Davies!' cried Arrowsmith, panicking now.
'Can't you see the man's mad? Stop him. You're
the law!'

'He *has* got a gun,' reminded Davies, who then
turned to Black. 'What are you going to do?'

'Simple. Your people have cleared out everybody in the path of this dam for several miles
downstream, right?'

Davies nodded.

'Well, I'll just shut off these valves,' he continued, beginning to shut the storm-sluice once more.
'Then I shall leave Mr Arrowsmith and his conscience together for a while. Don't worry about
me, though. I'll be along as soon as I've finished
shutting down the dam.'

For a moment Davies looked at Black closely.
He wasn't sure if he liked what he was getting into. Hasker was now teetering on the edge of panic

and would have run for it had Davies's restraining bulk not blocked the only exit.

Seeming to feel Davies's apprehension, Black sought to appease him. 'Look, as soon as Arrowsmith wants to tell us about everything he only has to shout. Then I'll come down again and take his story on his,' he indicated the newspaperman, 'recorder. Assuming I hear him call in the first place, that is.'

Again Davies looked at Black who though watching everyone's every move still managed to carry on with his task of shutting down the valves. Then Davies nodded. 'Ok,' he said, gruffly, 'but if this dam goes you're going to have one hell of a bill to pay.'

'You're all bluffing!' screamed Arrowsmith.

'You should ask our friend Hasker if I bluff or not,' suggested Black without halting in his work.

'For God's sake let's get out of here,' was Hasker's only reaction, however, and Arrowsmith looked very subdued.

With that the three began to leave and with them went any trace of confidence Arrowsmith had left. He finally snapped when Black announced, 'Good. That's the lot shut,' and strode for the doorway without a backward glance.

He didn't get as far as the doorway, however, for Arrowsmith was not of a mind to be left alone with the prospect of death looming in the very near future. Suddenly he cracked, issuing a tirade which, though long on threats, was short on duration, and it was only seconds before it ended in submission.

From their stance just outside the doorway, Davies and the newspaperman returned and over the next few minutes, interjected with unheeded pleas from Arrowsmith for them to open the valves, Black and the two men listened to a story which would completely shatter in public the man who they now saw shattered in private.

There was little for Black to find reassuring in what was said because only now did he fully realise the power and cunning his adversary had shown. But at least he had foiled one of Arrowsmith's plans when he had rightly got away from the man delivering the car at the inn. Arrowsmith had admitted it was this man who had wrecked the computer because they had feared what information it might contain.

As soon as Black was satisfied there was nothing major left for Arrowsmith to tell he unceremoniously untied the man and pushed him out onto the catwalk in the direction of the causeway beyond.

'The valves!' cried Arrowsmith, as he stumbled along the dam parapet. 'You haven't opened the valves.'

'What do you care whether they're open or shut,' said Black. 'You're safe now. Safe to face the courts,'

Beside him the newspaperman looked worried. 'Don't worry,' said Davies, seeing the same expression. The valves were only shut for a second-or-so.'

The newspaperman's expression didn't change.

'He shut them but then re-opened them immediately,' added the policeman. 'That was when I knew what our Mr Black was up to. Fortunately Arrowsmith was not in the frame of mind to think clearly enough to realise what was going on.'

On the way to the police vehicles located some way off the dam - and now joined by an assortment of heavy trucks - the little group passed some uniformed police who Davies instructed to finish up work in the valve-house.

'So the dam was never in any danger?' asked the newspaperman.

'Who can say with the age of these dams. With the valves shut it is quite probable it would have been rolled over by the water once it reached the top of the parapet. Perhaps before. It might have been days or just hours...' Black suddenly halted as they heard a loud noise behind them. They were just off the dam now but hundreds of yards from safety if it should *go*. Swiftly each one of them turned round, each one looking for any sign that the dam had started to breach. Black for his part held his breath.

'What was that?' said the newspaperman, asking the question on each man's lips.

Then came the answer as they heard over Davies's radio that the men in the valve-house had accidentally dropped one of the gas-bottles down the hatch to the second level.

'Keep going,' encouraged Davies, pounding his chest with his fist.

Then the group turned back again to continue their walk to the police cars.

'What will you do now?' asked Davies of Black.

'Difficult to say,' he responded. 'Continue in the same job, I suppose. The thing is Alland, and even Hasker, have shown me that there is a need for something more if people like Arrowsmith are to be stopped. Yes, I'll continue the old job but also spread the word about pollution a little louder.'

Davies looked up quickly at this. 'Beat the drum, you mean?'

Black halted and looked round and over the reservoir. It was almost dark now and he could see the arc-lamps shining above a raft of drums, the tops of which occasionally loomed into sight above the calm waters. They were almost surrounded by inflation bags now, placed there by what he now recognized from their uniforms as soldiers, busy as they operating from Gemini inflatable dinghies. Very soon they would have the chemical clear of the water and out of harm's way.

Or would they? thought Black. Might it not just end up on some dump, for someone later to build a children's school on in years to come? He didn't like to guess.

He turned back to Davies then. 'That's right,' he said slowly. 'The drum. We must continue to beat the drum.'

THE END